LEGACY

OF THE

DRAGON BONE FLUTE

Lord
Dance to
your own
song

A Novella By

M Todd Gallowglas

For Lisa
Thank you for taking a bunch of diamonds in the rough and making them SHINE!

ACKNOWLEDGEMENTS

As always, I want to thank my wife Robin. It's rare that a writer finds someone who knows the fine line between a soft caress and a slap upside the head to jumpstart me into writing. Robert, Mathew, and now Megan too: the greatest kids in the world that keep me full of stories and who think it's cool their dad is a writer – though I think Megan is still at the point where she thinks everything is cool. Again, the cats at the Starbucks in Lincoln, CA for keeping me well caffeinated. Simon, Henry, and Jose at DeVere's pub in Sacramento and Davis – I wrote the first words of fiction I got paid for at DeVere's, and it's been a cool ride ever since. All the great writers at the Genre Underground. Alyxx Duggin's, as always, your work is exquisite, thank you for putting the perfect face on Killian's story.

A very special thank you to "The Piano Guys." The last three quarters of this story probably wouldn't have happened if I hadn't had their music playing in my headphones. Don't know if they'll ever know how much they helped inspire this story, but I had to give a shout out in my own way.

Finally, thanks to my fans and readers who loved Elzibeth's story so much they demanded more Dragon Bone Flute. This was a fun one. Hope you all enjoy reading it even more than I enjoyed writing it, and that was quite a bit. I also hope you like Killian as much as you did Elzibeth. He's a different sort. And don't worry... Elzibeth will be back.

The one human in all the world of legends sat at the edge of a cliff, playing her flute as the sun set on the distant horizon, painting the sky red, yellow, and orange and the clouds blue and purple.

A dragon, one of the oldest and craftiest of all the great wyrms, glided toward the woman whose hair matched the brilliant sunset. Before touching bare earth, the dragon shifted forms, becoming human as it landed. The great wyrm waited politely until the woman finished her song, then it spoke.

"Magic is fading from the world of men."

"You say that as if it is a bad thing."

The wyrm considered this for a few moments. "You don't think so?"

The woman stared at the flute in her lap for a long while before she replied, "Magic had its time in my world. That time had passed long before me. Knowing magic brought me more sorrow than joy."

"But you are here."

"You wouldn't understand. You, with your centuries upon centuries of life. You, who watched kingdoms and empires rise and topple. You could not grasp the pain I felt at having touched the magic, having drawn the music of your kind to bring wonder into the world for such a short time, and then never know it for the rest of my life. Magic is wonderful. Magic is terrible. The world of men is better off without it."

"What of the world of legends, then?"

"It is better off without the world of men."

"*We cannot exist without a connection to the world of men,*" the great wyrm said. "*Without some small spark of magic in that realm, we will lose the tether that keeps us real.*"

"*What?*"

"*No one has told you, because it is not their place to trouble our honored guest. I am ancient, yet I still do not wish to fade into nothing.*"

"*You wish me to go back?*" the woman asked. "*Will I return as I am, young and beautiful, or as I was, hunched over and gray?*"

"*Neither,*" the great wyrm replied. "*If you were to return, you would die. You have lived among us beyond what your years in the world of men would allow.*"

"*Then why come to me?*"

"*I have watched your family. You have a grandson. He has that same spark within him that rests within you. He would be able to use the flute as you did.*"

"*And why would I place such a terrible burden upon anyone of my blood?*"

"*As I said, if magic fades completely from the world, the world of legends will fade into nothing. That includes you now. Are you so ready to meet your end? And it shall be an end. Not death. Just gone. Forever.*"

"*What would you have me do?*"

"*Give me the flute. I have power enough to send it to a place where he will find it.*"

"*What makes you so sure he'll play it?*"

"Because he has heard the stories about you, and more than anything else he yearns to be like you. He alone out of all your kin has your hair, your heart, and most of all, your love of song."

The woman placed the flute on the ground beside her. For a few moments she stroked the pale instrument.

"You can get this to him?"

"I can."

The woman kept her hand on the flute as she stared into the setting sun. The great wyrm gave no indication that his patience was wearing thin. He had a plan, and unlike most plans devised by dragonkind, this particular scheme did not have the luxury of centuries to come to fruition.

"What is his name?"

"Killian."

Finally, as the sun truly set, she took her hand away from the flute.

Without even the smallest bit of hurry, the wyrm took the flute and left.

The lady stared into the night sky of the world of legends, a black sea of multi-colored stars.

"I'm sorry, Killian," the woman said, after a time. "Gods and goddesses be with you."

Legacy of the Dragon Bone Flute

I

We all look back and search for those moments that define ourselves, the moments where we made a choice, and in making that choice, we affect all other choices to follow and we close off any chance of avoiding whatever fate comes with that choice. I didn't believe that then, back when I was young and believed myself immortal, as the young do, and had the luxury of believing that coincidence and chance controlled my destiny rather than taking responsibility for my actions. My name is Killian. I will not give you my family name, for I have family that survives me. While I hope this account finds its way into one of my descendants' hands, as my grandmother's journal found its way into mine, I cannot be sure. And so, I will protect my family from the choices I have made, and the enemies that came along with those choices.

Now, I was speaking of moments and choices that change the course of our lives. If any one moment could be said to be the turning point in my life, I'd like to be able to say it was when I decided – against, I might add, the wishes and warnings of my parents, grandparents, siblings, and cousins – to explore the abandoned farmstead of my great grandmother. But it was not that day when I decided I was old enough – this happened to be my ten-and-fifth naming day – to command my own fate, and sneak out early one morning with the forbidden farmstead as my solitary goal. It's true, the moment I left the yard, walking through the gate without being called back, was a shift in my destiny, where all further actions and choices moved me toward becoming a hero, trickster, villain, madman, wanderer, fugitive, prince, hermit, and friend to legends, and all that before my ten-and-sixth name day.

But it was not that day, and it was not that choice.

The major snows had melted, and most of the village had gathered together in the tavern as was the tradition when spring began to creep back into the world. And as I neared my ten-and-fifth naming day, I sat alone in a corner. Now I was an oddity in the village. For whatever reason, I'd been born at a time of scarce births. Then several hard winters in a row had claimed the other children close to my age. So I considered myself too old to any longer tolerate sitting at the long table with the children – the eldest of them was three years younger than I was. Oh I'd tried to join with the adults, but I was not quite old enough for them to actually count me one of them. I'm sure my small stature didn't help. Without any peers close to my own age, the corner was the place I hid, mostly so I wouldn't suffer the humiliation of having my small beer taken away and then get herded back to shepherd over the children.

Alone and melancholy, trying to take solace in having a tankard of the weakest brew offered in the tavern, it took me a moment to realize someone was standing next to me. I looked up. My uncle, called Daft Uncle Ian by the village when he wasn't listening – even by those who weren't related to him – looked down at me.

"May I sit?" Uncle Ian asked.

I scooted over, making room on the bench. It took a bit for him to settle down next to me. He'd injured his leg in a war long past. Most of the village thought that's where he'd also gone daft, that he'd damaged his brain in the same cavalry charge that had crippled his leg.

Once he sat, bad leg stretched out before him, he took a long drink from his mug, stared into the fire and began to hum. I recognized the tune, "The Beggar King." It was one of my favorites. Before he finished even the first verse, he stopped humming and spoke to me.

"We're quite the pair," Uncle Ian said. "They all think us both wandering away from our senses. Don't bother arguing. I know what they say about me. And you…well…you might say that they think you're a bit daft for overstepping yourself and trying to join them before they invite you as has always been the way of it."

He took a sip from his tankard. I took a sip from mine.

"Here," he said, handing me his drink and taking mine. "I'm fool enough to have had one of these, much less be starting on my third. None of this lot will help me home tonight, and I've no need to be stumbling around in the dark trying to remember which home is mine. Just be sure you don't let your parents catch you with that mug of Highhill Dark."

"No, sir," I said.

Then I took a drink, a healthy-sized one.

The full flavor of it washed over my tongue and settled in my stomach with a weight that was at the same time warm and comforting and nauseating. A few moments later, my head swam. I could definitely grow to like this.

"You think they won't let you join them because you're still too young," Uncle Ian said.

I nodded.

"Not true." He drank. "They're afraid of you."

"Me?" I asked, my voice rising more than it normally would have, even considering my surprise at Uncle Ian's statement. I lowered it to a whisper. "Why would anyone be afraid of me?"

"You know that song you like so much?" he asked. "The one you're always playing or singing as you go about your chores and such."

"The Beggar King?" I asked. I had several such, but I was sharp enough, even back then, to see some things right in front of my face.

"The Beggar King," he replied. "It was her favorite song."

"Whose favorite song?" I asked.

12

"You remind them of her. Too much, you remind them. Of her."

"Who, her?"

Ian leaned close to my ear. "Heeeerrr." His breath tickled my ear and neck. His breath stank of beer and stew.

I thought for what might have been a few moments. Thinking had suddenly become a more difficult task than I remembered it being.

"You have the look of her," Uncle Ian said, "More than anyone in the family. Short, wiry, shock of flame on your head that some people call hair. I've heard my parents whisper that you have her manner, too. Stubborn, proud, and a flat refusal to let anyone dictate your life for you."

"Oh." I took another drink of my Highhill Dark, though not as healthy a swallow as my first taste. "That her."

Uncle Ian was speaking of my great-grandmother Elzibeth. She and my great grandfather Frances had come to the village when they were only slightly older than I was. They'd picked a plot of land on the very edge of the village and settled there. Stories about them from that point disagree. One of the most fanciful is the reason most folk think of Uncle Ian as Daft Uncle Ian.

"I saw it happen, you know," he said.

"I know," I said. "You've told me before."

"So I have," Uncle Ian said, "but I haven't told you everything. I haven't ever told anyone everything."

I took another drink, bracing myself for the story to come. Everyone knew the best thing to do was to sit quietly when Ian started in on this, let him get on with his tale, and pray that it was one of the shorter versions he told.

"It was shortly after I'd come home from the war. My leg still hurt with stabbing pains all the time back then, not the simple ache I feel now. I was up late, biting my lips to keep from whimpering and crying so my parents could sleep. They took good care of me and didn't need their crippled son keeping them up at all hours. It was a warm night, so I had my shutters open. I might as well enjoy the summer breeze and the peace that comes with the quiet of the world at sleep."

Ian took a drink of the small beer he'd taken from me.

"You've heard this before," Ian said, "all about Daft Uncle Ian and how he saw dragons that carried Grandmother Elzibeth away. But you've never heard it with that," he pointed to the tankard he'd given me. "That's why you're pretending to listen, so you can enjoy that tasty bit of drink. But here's what I've never told anyone. Before the dragons came, I heard music. Flute music."

I sat up straight and turned to give Uncle Ian my full attention. This was a new part of the story.

"Got your attention, did that?" he asked. "I thought it might. Have you ever wondered why so many of the older folk in the village seem to shy away whenever you pick up that flute you bought from the peddler a few years ago?"

I shook my head.

"They fear it, you playing any musical instrument, but most of all a flute."

"Why?"

He smiled at me in a way that I'd never seen Uncle Ian smile before. It was the smile that someone gave to someone else who was so sick or injured that they might never recover, a smile while trying to spare the terrible news as long as possible. He reached for the tankard of Highhill Dark. I gave it over without protest. As much as I enjoyed the effect and was even growing accustomed to the potent taste, young people of the village, even when they were close to their ten-and-fifth name day, did not disobey and disrespect their elders.

"You've gotten fairly good." He took a long drink of the Highhill Dark. "That's even more reason why you scare them."

I tried to wait patiently, but he seemed unwilling to continue. I tried to content myself by listening to other conversations, but no one was close enough for me to hear them clearly above the din of the rest of the tavern. I hummed through a complete round of, "The Beggar King" and two other songs quietly to myself. After that, I waited for what seemed like forever, I couldn't help but speak up.

"Uncle Ian, why does my flute playing scare them?"

He leaned close and whispered "Listen well, young Killian. I will not tell this again. I probably shouldn't now, but I think you should know what kind of door you've opened and are getting ready to walk through."

"Does it have something to do with you hearing flute music the night Grandmother Elzibeth got carried off?"

"You're getting ahead of my story, boy." Uncle Ian glared at me even as he drank again. "Don't ever get ahead of the story. That's the problem with you musicians. Everything is so fast for you. Put everything together in a song that takes only a few minutes, and everything repeats over and over and over. You've got no appreciation for the beginning, middle, and end of things."

"I'm sorry Uncle Ian." Part of me couldn't believe I was apologizing for this. He was on the edge, and I suspect he hadn't been honest with me when he'd handed me the Highhill Dark. I should have walked away. I almost did. But then that bit about the flute music held me to the bench. I'd heard him tell this story countless times, but this was the first time he'd ever mentioned any music. "I'll listen quietly, and let you tell the story the proper way.

"Good on you then, lad." Uncle Ian patted me on the back. "Good on you."

We sat there for a while, him drinking, me waiting. And I waited quietly, so that I didn't upset him and lose this tale. I feared if Uncle Ian walked away from this telling, I'd never have a chance to hear it again.

Finally, he put the tankard aside, put his arm around me, and drew me in close.

"I heard it floating down from Grandmother Elzibeth's cottage. It was beautiful…more haunting and beautiful than anything I've ever heard…not from any minstrel coming through on his way from one place to another…beautiful enough to break your heart with the knowing that magic had come to the world and the world had scorned it…even killed a part of it…and then…the magic left…fled really…and all because we chased it away.

"And while I heard that song, my leg stopped hurting…for the first time since I fell from that horse, my leg stopped hurting. I could walk. When I got outside of the cottage, I found I could run.

"That's when I saw them…coming down from the sky…even in the moonlight I saw them…one green as any emerald and one blue as any sapphire…almost as if they radiated the colors of their scaly hides…then the music stopped.

"Pain flared in my leg again. I fell to the road and rolled behind a cart. I nearly bit my tongue in half to keep from crying out. The last thing I wanted was to attract

17

their attention, but that also didn't stop me from watching from the shadows under that cart. I watched them pull the roof off Grandmother Elzibeth's cottage, set that roof down, reach into her cottage, pick her up, and carry her off. The green one scooped her up out of the cottage and placed her right down on the blue one, just in front of its wings.

"And that's the last anyone ever saw of Grandmother Elzibeth. And that's why we moved the village. Don't let anyone else tell you otherwise, boy. Though none else will admit it, I was not the only one to see dragons that night. There was much talk of it during the days we moved. Small-minded folk, most the people here are, thinking that moving half a day south would save them if the dragons ever came back looking to cause mischief, or worse. I knew better from my travels, but they wouldn't hear any of my advice, and it's not like I was in any shape with my leg the way it is to move on myself."

He took another drink, finishing the mug.

"But you'd heard all that before," Uncle Ian said, "about the dragons and such, isn't that right, boy?"

"Yes, sir," I replied.

"But not the music."

"No, sir," I said. "Not about the music."

"And there's something else," Uncle Ian said. He leaned in very close and whispered so low I could barely hear him. "Do you want to hear it?"

I nodded.

"As those two dragons flew up into the night, I saw something drop. I couldn't tell what, but I saw something small, flashing white in the moonlight fall from the sky moments after they rose out of sight. After that, sometimes, when the wind was just right, a solitary note would hang on the wind, and my leg wouldn't hurt. First happened the day after they took her. That was part of the reason they fled, the cowards. That one note pushed them over the edge of reason. I argued against it. They wouldn't hear me. Silly, superstitious folk. Not that I blame them overly much. I'd been like them before I left for the wars. Wish I hadn't. Then I wouldn't have this leg, and I wouldn't know what idiots my family and neighbors are, that I'd been too, once upon a time."

"What's going on here?" a deep voice asked.

Both Uncle Ian and I jumped.

My father stood behind us, glaring down.

"What nonsense are you filling my son's head with?" my father asked.

"Nothing, Father," I replied. "He was just telling me his story," I added with as bored a tone as I could manage, "again."

Father looked at Uncle Ian and me, back and forth several times. The disapproval of that gaze pressed down upon me. When dealing with my uncle, I was, like many of the children of the village, caught between two expectations: Do not spend too much time with Daft Uncle Ian, and do not under any circumstances be rude to your elders.

"Well, your mother's tired," Father said at last. "We're going home."

"Yes, Father," I said. "Thank you for telling me the story, Uncle Ian."

Uncle Ian nodded. Father led me away. Mother was waiting for us by the door.

"How many times have I told you?" Father asked. "Stay away from your Uncle Ian."

I knew he didn't really expect an answer. Even at ten and four, I'd gotten fairly good at understanding the difference between questions my elders expected me to answer and the questions they were merely asking to drive home a point I should have already gotten through my thick skull and put into practice. I just kept my eyes on the floor and nodded.

When we joined my mother outside, Father cuffed me on the back of the head so hard I took a couple of staggering steps forward to keep my balance.

"Look at me, Killian!" Father snapped.

I quickly wiped the welling tears from my eyes before turning to face him.

"Your Uncle can be charming and warm and exciting with his stories of dragons and his adventures during the war," Father said. "But he's also dangerous. Best not to talk to him so he can't be putting crazy ideas into your head."

"Yes, Father," I said.

Father flicked me on the nose. "Stop giving me the answers you think I want to hear, especially now that you're becoming a young man. There's no telling what he might try to talk you into doing for him. Promise me you won't do anything foolish."

"I know, Father," I said, blinking from the pain. "I know what my responsibilities are and where my duty lies."

What I didn't say was that Daft Uncle Ian had treated me more like an adult this evening than my father ever had. I also learned long ago when to keep the hole under my nose closed.

Daft Uncle Ian hadn't talked me into doing anything, but my father certainly had.

II

Even before the sun rose on the morning of my ten-and-fifth name day, I crept out of my window, because I didn't want to risk the stairs creaking as I left. Father was a light sleeper, as I'd learned the first time I'd tried sneaking out at night. After that one time, I'd practiced climbing up and down anything I could when no one was watching so that I could get out of my window. I doubt my father thought me brave enough to try it. Much of that had to do with the appearance that I put up to keep from being reminded that I was just a scrawny little slip of a boy.

The village was quiet as I jogged away from my home. I had a bedroll, lantern, and waterskin slung over my shoulders under my cloak. My pockets held my box of fishing line, hooks, and flint and steel. And the day before I'd gone into the kitchen and filched bread, fruit, and some cheese. All were tucked safely away in the bottom of my pack. I was confident I had everything I could possibly need for whatever this adventure brought me.

I escaped the village without notice. At the time, I thought I'd made some grand escape, slipping out because I was so very clever and cunning. Looking back, I realize it's likely that those few people who were up and about before the sun rose assumed that I was up and about for some errand or other for my parents.

By the time the village was out of sight behind the hills, I was skipping and whistling a tune. By midmorning, I had my flute out and played it as loud and as strong as I ever had. Uncle Ian was right about the townsfolk and my playing: While they never said anything, and likely never would, I knew by the way the elders wouldn't quite look at me and they shied away whenever they saw the flute in my hands that they didn't approve.

My playing made my feet seem lighter and the road seem shorter. I didn't feel it as the day grew long, and much sooner than I expected the sun hung low in western sky and I could see the remains of the old village. I stopped playing when the first cottages came into view.

Walking toward the houses, I took in the sight of the abandoned village. For having been neglected for the better part of two generations, the old village was in surprisingly good repair. Here and there a roof had fallen in. Weeds had sprouted up between the boards of almost every porch. Two of the houses had collapsed in on themselves completely. In nearly all other ways, with a bit of hard work, the old village could be habitable again.

My jovial wonder at the old village changed shortly after I walked between the first homes. The place wasn't in as good repair as it had seemed from the hill above. The stench of rotting wood permeated the air to such an extent that I had to wrap my scarf around my mouth and nose to keep from gagging. White paint on the cottages had gone to a sickly gray color and was chipped and peeling everywhere. Broken windows gaped at me like mouths with jagged glass teeth waiting to gnash my limbs if I wandered too close. That a few of the windows still had unbroken glass, streaked and muddy, made the others seem all the more sinister.

I pulled my scarf down. After a few moments I got used to the smell and tried to play a bit to liven my mood. Birds cried out and erupted out of windows and up from collapsed roofs, and a fox burst out of a bush not five paces away. I stopped playing as I let my breathing and heartbeat slow down to a relatively normal pace. I tucked my flute away and continued on in quiet.

Since Uncle Ian had spun his tale for me at the first gathering of spring, I wasn't sure I believed him. I wanted to, and even deep down I believed him as much as anyone who has one foot over the threshold of adulthood while the other foot remained firmly planted in childhood with every intention of fighting to stay there. But the truth was that I didn't really believe the story of dragons and all that. This journey had been as much about moving beyond the dreams and fancies of my childhood as anything else.

Then I came to the far end of the old village and saw a roofless cottage. Not a cottage where the roof had collapsed in. I'd already seen a handful of those. Even in my village such a thing happened once every few winters – so much snow would fall that one of the roofs wouldn't hold against its weight. No, this cottage simply had no roof, and it was in a worse state of repair than all the others. One wall had crumbled and rotted away to nearly nothing. The chimney looked like an arm weakly reaching up to prove that it still had strength. A tree grew above the walls from within the cottage. The roof lay fifty paces away in the center of a field, grasses growing up all around it. Staring at this strange scene, gaze shifting slowly back and forth between the ruined cottage and the roof, my mind envisioned dragons descending from the sky and pulling the roof up, just as the old story went.

Without even realizing it, my feet took me closer to the ruined structure. Mouth agape, eyes wide, I approached as if I was some pilgrim arriving at the temple of some long-forgotten god. In many ways, so much mystery, wonder, and fear surrounded Grandmother Elzibeth that she might as well have been a goddess. We spoke of her mostly in whispers, awe clear in our voices, usually remembering her as kind and benevolent, but also hoping, praying, that speaking her name would not gain her attention and summon her back.

Soon I stood only a few paces from her fabled cottage.

Even over the span of so many years, I can still remember the argument I had with myself in that moment. One part of my mind spoke with Father's voice, telling me that I should return to my home, do my chores, and see to the responsibilities of the here and now. The other side of my mind spoke from a place deeper within me, that part of me that longed to roam the world beyond the horizon, likely the same yearning given to me by Grandmother Elzibeth that had caused her to commune with dragons, and the same yearning that had set Uncle Ian's feet to the road in search of adventures. The two voices rattled back and forth between my ears, pushing and pulling my heart this way and that.

Even with as much as I wanted the adventure, I couldn't help but consider this roofless husk that had once been a home, and there was also Uncle Ian's shattered leg, so Father's voice began to win out. While I might very well find the beginnings of an adventure, in every story I'd ever heard – even the ones I made up to amuse myself during my chores – being at the center of an adventure came with as much a cost, or more, than it did rewards.

I was about to turn my back on Grandmother Elzibeth's cottage and return home, when a breeze rose from behind me, weak at first, barely noticeable, but it grew and grew until I felt the warmth of it brush at my ears and the hairs on my neck. I shivered. Then I heard it – a musical note. Now as I close my eyes I can still feel that note reaching out to me, and I do mean that I felt the note rather than heard the note, for it came from within the cottage and was so soft, with the wind whistling about, I couldn't possibly have heard it.

Again, my feet were moving without me being conscious of making any choice. That part of me shared only by Grandmother Elzibeth and Uncle Ian needed to see what had made that perfect sound.

A few moments and purposeful strides later, I stood in the center of that cottage, that temple to the patron goddess of my family line, staring at a pale flute perched in the most unlikely of places: between two branches of the tree growing as if it was a shrine within this temple, sent by the goddess herself to present me with this instrument.

The breeze rose again. The branches of the tree waved with the wind. As the tree moved, so did the flute, catching the wind at just the right angle, and that note sounded again for the briefest of moments.

My heart both soared and shattered at the same time.

I thought I'd known music before, but now I realized that what I'd heard had been watered down small beer and what I was hearing now was Highhill Dark. Or, at least that was the best comparison my young mind could make at the time. I can give several dozen comparisons now, but that would be dishonest to the story of the young man I was in that moment.

The note trailed off to silence as the breeze died down, leaving a hollow world behind.

Without a single thought or moment of care, I walked over to the tree, reached up, and snatched the flute down. I held it as if it were some fragile thing made of glass. It was smooth, smoother than any wood I'd ever known, despite being completely unpolished. A cool tingling tickled my palm and fingers where they touched the thing. Despite this, I turned the instrument round and round in my hands, looking it over from all angles. When I'd first seen it, I thought the off-white color was just a trick of the shadows of the tree. Now, with it in my hand, I saw that its color was not a trick of the light. As I studied and held it, I realized this off-whitish flute was not wood, rather it had been carved from an incredibly long, thin bone, a bone that had come from no animal I had ever seen. My imagination soared through all the stories and songs of mythic and magical creatures I'd ever heard the minstrels, troubadours, and gleeman recount in the village tavern. Some of those animals were as frightening as they were amazing, and I nearly put the flute back when the wind grew again. This time, the flute did not echo through the ruined cottage, and my world was lacking in the absence of that sweet, wonderful note. Having heard that solitary note once and having it absent now, my chest tightened and my mouth went dry with the need to hear an entire song played by this strange, wonderful, and slightly frightening thing.

I lifted the flute, but paused a moment with it bare inches from my face. Licking my lips, I swallowed as best I could with my dry mouth as I stared at the flute, considering: Touching the bone of some strange creature with my hands was one thing; actually putting it against my mouth was another matter entirely, one that I can say, looking back over all these years, did give me a moment's pause…but only a moment.

Hesitation gone, I placed it to my lips, put my fingers above the holes while caressing it with my thumbs, and began to play.

I played the only song that seemed fitting. Her favorite, and one of mine.

"The Beggar King" is a light, airy tune that never fails to lift my spirits. As I always did, every time I reached the chorus, I imagined a female voice singing along:

> *"I'd rather be a beggar than a king,*
> *And I'll tell you the reason why.*
> *A king can never be free from a beggar,*
> *Nor half as happy as I!"*

Who was the girl? Whichever young lady whose heart I might one day happen to capture. At ten and five, it didn't matter that I likely hadn't met her yet; she was probably some girl from a neighboring village I'd meet at one of the great feast gatherings. It didn't matter that I didn't know her. If she didn't know the words to "The Beggar King," I would teach her.

I played the song twice, enjoying the playing of it far more than I had enjoyed playing any other song in all the days of my short life. The spirit of the tune filled me. Truly a life of wandering freedom would be preferable to any trade or profession that might shackle me to a life of tedium, even if that shackle happened to be a throne. A prison is a prison no matter the look of it, and some men were simply born to wander free, spreading stories and songs across the world.

The song ended. I took the flute from my lips. The silence in the world pressed down on me. Oh, sound abounded: birds in the distance, the wind through the ruins of the village, and crickets chirping. But the absence of that flute's breath of life filling the empty places between those other sounds might as well have been utter silence. Each moment when there was nothing – the wind died, the birds quieted, and the chirping paused for the briefest of moments – stretched for a lifetime, and my heart ached with loneliness and longing.

Breathing slowly, I opened my eyes. I didn't remember closing them. I found I was no longer in the husk that had been Grandmother Elzibeth's house. I was now standing in the center of the road, a good distance from the old village.

"Thank you," a voice said, above and behind me.

I swallowed, turned around very, very slowly, not sure I wanted to know what had spoken.

I didn't want to know.

I screamed.

III

"Again?" the great shimmering image of a dragon said. "You humans are such an excitable people." It cocked its head to the side and then stretched its neck out, lowering that massive head to look at me somewhat thoughtfully. "Or perhaps it's just a trait you inherited from her."

The dragon was massive, wings stretching into the sky and tail worming its way back through the houses of the old village. I could sort of see through it in most places, though parts of its body shone enough so that they almost seemed solid.

"Well, little human," the dragon asked, "which do you think it is?"

I tried to respond. More like I made a sound like, "Gaworraaack."

The dragon pulled back a bit, cocked its head to the other side, and then blinked several times.

"I'm unfamiliar with that language," it said. Then it spoke very slowly. "Do... you... know... these... words? Nod... if... you... do."

Rubbing one hand over my face, I closed my eyes. I prayed that this might be some strange figment of my mind trying to fill the absence of the flute's music. For a brief moment, I considered playing another song, but then if this was some trick of my mind to cope with no longer having the sound of one song filling the space of the world around me, I didn't want to think about how terrible a vision I would have after the loss of a second such song.

Opening my eyes again, the creature was still there.

I nodded.

"Good," the dragon said. "That is something. Do you speak this language?"

Being small of stature made me a bit overly timid in new situations until I could get my bearings, but once I could take stock of a situation and understand a bit of what was going on, my timidity tended to fade quickly. I cared not a bit for this creature's tone.

"Yes," I replied. "I speak language good."

The dragon's head drew back, snout pressed against its neck, nostrils flared, and eyes narrowed.

"You do not need to be rude." The dragon spoke with a tone of reproach similar to my father when reprimanding my behavior.

Nobody likes being spoken down to, and being smaller of stature than some children in my home several years my junior, meant that I also had to endure many people talking down to me. Gods and goddesses, this was my ten-and-fifth name day, and I'd not have anyone speaking to me as a lesser.

I stood up straight, put my hands on my hips, glared right up at that spectral dragon, and replied, "Nor do you."

The dragon's mouth opened, closed, and opened again. Had I'd pushed too far? I'd thought that since it hadn't killed me already, it didn't want to harm me – the pride of my youth had blinded me into thinking that our interaction would stay civil no matter how I behaved. Ah, the power of hindsight. Then it placed its head on the ground, snout not four paces from me, and I could see that several of its fangs were easily as long as I was tall.

"How have I been rude?" it asked in a whisper that dried my mouth.

"Well…uh…" I started, no longer under the illusion that just because it hadn't harmed me, things wouldn't change if I didn't choose my words with great care. "You see…Si…Um, I beg your pardon, but are you male or female? You are the first dragon I've ever met, and so I have no basis to know which honorific I should use to address you."

The massive head cocked to the side again. A long moment passed before it replied.

"I was female in life."

"Well, ma'am," I said, and gave a bow. "I would say that it's not terribly polite to come upon people by surprise and give them the fright of their lives. I'm sure that dragons do not have much to fear in the world, but men, especially young men as myself," I gestured over my smallish frame, "are not so hearty, and the world is full of dangers."

"I suppose you are correct," the dragon said. "I apologize for startling you."

"Thank you, ma'am," I said. "Apology accepted. I apologize for taking a terse and short tone with you."

"Accepted as well." Its head rose again, and it sat back on its haunches, drawing its wings close in to its body. "You remind me very much of your grandmother."

I blinked at that. "You know Grandmother Elzibeth."

"Well, she wasn't a grandmother back then, but yes, I knew her. She made the flute you just played. Carved it out of one of my toe bones."

I stared down at the instrument in my hands. "Really?" It certainly did explain a lot of what had happened when I played it. "Really?"

"Indeed," the dragon replied. "That is part of what drew me here, occasionally hearing the hint of a note from it, though that has only been recently. I can feel another part of myself nearby as well. Even after death, I had been whole for so long…now…now, I feel myself scattered across…"

Her voice trailed off. She lifted her head and sniffed at the air. I could hear the succession of sharp intakes of breath. I recall wondering why a ghost would need to sniff the air. But, I suppose that knowing little of ghosts and dragons, much less ghostly dragons, I should do well not to make such rash assumptions.

"Scattered across?" I prompted, hoping that she would continue.

The dragon's body shimmered and seemed to ripple, and in the next moment she was gone.

"Hello?" I called. "Come back!"

I waited a few moments, and when she did not return, I called out again. Still, she did not return.

Remembering what had summoned her before, I placed the flute to my lips and drew in a deep breath to play again.

Before I could sound the first note, a finger and thumb clamped onto my ear and twisted it just enough to get my attention and pull me off balance.

IV

"You worried your mother sick," my father's voice snapped behind me. "And I told you not to let your uncle talk you into doing anything foolish. Well, I suppose you did obey me, in a way. In coming here, you went well beyond foolish and straight to stupid."

Normally, my father's tone and his grip on my ear would have cowed me into submission. More than that, he would have kept his vice-like fingers clamped onto my ear for the entire journey home. Well, that had been before I stood my ground against a spectral dragon, the memory of which does not fill me with the same dread as does confronting my father on anything. Odd isn't it? Even as I write these words, years and decades after the events occurred with my father now likely rotting in his grave, my chest tightens at the thought of his displeasure, and even as I consider what I did next, I feel myself reacting to my father as I might have at any other moment save for that one, my eye – the left one – is twitching, my mouth is getting dry, and my breathing is getting shallow. Even the quill I'm writing with shakes in my hands. But…I digress.

Now, because I was set the task to polish Father's boots by the fire the night before endweek gathering, and having done this chore for well over two years, I happened to know that the leather where his foot meets his shin is thin – thin and soft – just the way he likes it. When the peddlers come every spring and autumn, Mother tries to get him to buy a new pair. Father won't hear anything of it. These boots do him just fine; besides, he's finally, finally gotten them broken in just right.

Just right for me to bring the heel of my boot down on that soft spot.

Which I did.

Hard.

Now, I didn't have hard-soled boots at that time. I was still growing, so the expense of such footwear would have been silly. Perhaps in a year or two I could look forward to a pair, but not yet. So, my foot wasn't going to cause Father as much harm as it could have, not that I'd wanted to really hurt him. I just wanted him to let go of my ear. Which he did, and gave the most boyish cry of surprise I'd ever heard from him.

The moment my ear was loose of his fingers, I scampered away from him.

"You little…" I heard him growl under his breath. The boyish surprise had given way to the quiet fatherly fury I was used to.

I spun in place.

"Stop!" I said, and thrust my hand out toward him.

Father had been coming after me, and he had to stop short to keep from getting hit in the face, but not by my hand. I still had Grandmother Elzibeth's flute. It stretched out a good ways from my fingers, wavering right under Father's nose.

His hand came up, and he drew it back, preparing to swat the flute away. Then he seemed to take it in as he adjusted his hand before striking. The familiar ruddy hue of his face paled, becoming not too dissimilar to the ashen off-white of the flute. His eyes seemed like they were trying to scrunch closed and widen at the same time. Staring down the length of my arm and the flute, watching my father's reaction made me want to laugh. He was one of the handful of men everyone came to when they needed advice, a dispute mediated, or some problem solved, and now here he was, stunned silent with fear over this little thing I pointed at him. I choked down a laugh but couldn't keep my lips from creeping into a smile. His attention turned from the flute to me, and I think that smile might have disturbed him more.

"Stop," I repeated.

I drew in a deep breath and let it out to see what Father would do. He stood for a moment, blinking at me, gaze shifting from me to the flute and back again. As he did so, my momentary resolve began to fade. Finally, after a few dozen heartbeats that seemed to be harder the longer we stood there staring at each other, Father took a step back…then another…then a third. As the distance between us grew, I lowered my arm.

His cheeks loosened, he rolled his shoulders as the tension left them, and his eyes seemed to agree on how much they wanted to be open. He still seemed pale, but his breathing returned to normal and he lowered his hand.

"It's my name day, Father," I said. "My ten-and-fifth. Please, let me have this adventure on this day. If you must keep me under your thumb and heel all the other days of my life because you think I'm too small and Mother thinks her precious little man is too fragile for the world, fine. I can live with that any other day. I already have. And I will again for the rest of my life. Just give me this one day. One adventure. Today." I paused, chewed my lower lip, and took a deep breath before I leaned forward, and added, "Please?"

Father crossed his arms and gave me the deep breath he exhales when considering what consequences I should suffer for whatever actions he feels warrants correction. He opened his mouth. I held up my hand.

"Before you say anything," I said, "answer me one question. What happened to you on your fifth-and-ten name day?"

Father smiled and gave a brief chuckle. His gaze shifted toward the horizon, and a wistful smile that crept onto his face. He looked that way every time he thought of his ten-and-fifth name day,

"I met your mother at the spring day celebration," he said. "My life changed forever."

"Right," I said. "Everyone thinks that their life is supposed to change forever on their fifth-and-ten name day. You're one of the few that actually happened to. I want my fifth-and-ten name day to mean as much to me as yours did to you. I want to look back when I have a son of my own and be able to tell him: My life changed forever on that day." I paused, drew in a deep gulp of air for I'd made my plea in a single breath, and added once more, "Please?"

Father shook his head, and the wistful smile broke into a wide grin.

"It seems my son is no longer a boy," he said. "You may not have grown in size, but the little boy is gone. It's hard to argue with a young man of conviction when he makes valid points." Father shook his head. "You come back in one piece, or your fifth-and-ten name day just may be the day my life ends forever, and if not, I'll likely wish it had. Even if she doesn't kill me, your mother will never forgive me."

"Yes, sir," I said. "I'll be careful."

"I seriously doubt that," Father said. "Just try not to be stupid."

He turned and took a few steps before looking back over his shoulder.

"I can't imagine I'll be able to talk you into dropping that thing," he gestured to the flute, "into someplace dark and deep. You're coming into your own, that much is clear. So, I won't give you any orders or commands about it, but please by all the gods and goddesses that look down upon us, do not let the others in the village see it. You'll have a hard enough time with them for a few months for having come up here. That thing," again, gesturing to the flute, "will cause you no end of grief from the elders, and that's if they find out you have it. Angels and demons alike protect us if they ever see or hear you playing it."

"Yes, Father," I said. "Be careful heading home in the dark."

"I will," he said, and his smile grew. "Besides, it may have been a few years, but this is not the first time I've made this journey in the dark. I know the way."

With a final nod, he headed back toward home at a brisk pace. I watched Father until he was out of sight, swallowed by the growing darkness. Part of me still can't believe that he allowed me to stay, that my words had moved him. I stood there for a time, even after I couldn't see Father any longer, shaking my head and laughing quietly to myself.

As the dark of true night approached, I gathered firewood and set myself to coaxing it to flame. Once the fire grew large enough to warm me against the chill of the early spring night and I ate about half of the food I'd brought, I placed the flute to my lips and began to play.

I played most of the way through the night, trying to get the spectral dragon to return.

I started with "The Beggar King." Again, as I played, I felt the power of that song wander around me, calling for distant lands, to travel as I would, calling no man master. When I finished the song, I found myself and my fire in the middle of the road leading out of the old village. Truly, I wasn't actually surprised by that. Well, the fire was a surprise, but not the fact that I'd moved again. Deep down, in the secret place inside me where my heart and mind mingled to create new songs, I'd known it was going to happen. Still, the fire moving with me was surprising.

Without batting my eyes – alright, I did look around for a few moments, but no more than just a few before I placed the flute back to my lips – I played another song.

Then another.

And another.

At first, I played lively songs, jigs and reels that danced alongside the sparks from my fire. Then, as the night grew colder and the flames died down, my songs turned somber and sorrowful. Finally, when only the barest of flames limped up from the last of my logs, I played one last dirge. When I finished the song, I looked around.

No dragon, spectral or otherwise.

I carefully made my way back to Grandmother Elzibeth's cottage and gathered my pack and bedroll from where I'd left them.

While returning to what was left of the fire, the darkness of the night pressed down on me. The eerie sense of strangeness from the buildings with no people living in them, seemingly watching me as I passed, made me feel the interloper. I felt judged for disturbing the stillness of this place. I had never felt so alone in all the days of my young life. Suddenly, I yearned for my father to return and force me home. I looked to the stars, at those islands of gossamer pinpricks in a sea of black. The courage and spirit I'd felt when standing up to Father and arguing my case was gone. I was no longer the brave hero of the legend of my fifth-and-ten name day. Now I was just scrawny, short, and just plain tiny Killian, jumping and starting at any strange sound. For a short time, I considered following Father. If I hurried, I might make it back to my bed before morning's light.

Just before I kicked the fire completely out, the wind rose. Not the cold, biting wind of winter struggling to remain in the world just a little while longer. Rather, the warm wind of later spring heralding summer's approach. It had been the same wind that had caused the flute to play earlier. I'd been so intrigued by the music I'd heard that I'd entirely missed the quality of the wind. This time, music did not come upon the breeze. How could it, as I'd moved the flute and so it could not catch the wind. The world seemed an emptier place, not having music dancing and skipping on that breeze.

I tossed fresh wood on the fire, wrapped my cloak and blanket around me, and I lifted the flute one last time that night to my lips.

This song wasn't anything I'd ever played before or based on any tune I'd heard. I played of the man I wanted to be. I played of being the man who stood up to my father, stood up to anyone and anything that might try to place limitations upon me. I played of guile and cunning and cleverness and wit, for that is how I'd trapped Father into leaving me here. These old buildings could judge me all they wished, and that sky above could try and press down upon me to make me feel smaller than I ever had before. Let them try! In truth, they were my prize. I had bested Father and made him relent. For the first time, I had come out victorious. Yes, it was a victory, the sweetest victory in my short life. My song soared, telling the rotting homes, the vast sky, and the dark, cold night that they were not my father's equals. The flames of the fire jumped and danced and reveled in the power of my music, pushing the darkness and cold away. Father had not broken me. These lesser things would not break me. I put all this into my song. A song I had never played before. A song I would never play again.

I had no idea how long the song went on, but when I finally pulled the flute from my lips, the fire snuffed out as if buried with dirt. The song had kept the flames alive long after the fuel had been spent. Not even enough embers remained for the slightest tendril of smoke to rise to the sky.

In my song's absence, the night tried to press down on me again.

I snickered. It had no power over me.

Pulling my cloak and blanket around me a little tighter, I tucked the flute under one arm and lay down to sleep without even the slightest sliver of fear in my heart.

V

When I woke the next morning, mist rose from the grass. Dew had soaked through my cloak. Shivers immediately wracked my body, and my teeth chattered so rapidly that my jaw ached. I stood up, stamped my feet, and rubbed my hands together. The sun wasn't even halfway above the horizon. Gods and goddesses, while I'd been up this early many a morning for chores, I'd always woken up in my warm bed. I'd never imagined how much of a difference that would make.

Well, nothing to be done but try to get my fire going again.

I wandered through the remains of the old village, gathering up any wood that looked anywhere near being dry. I had little luck. Some of the larger pieces were dry underneath, which would be fine, if by some miracle I could get the kindling to take a spark and catch.

After a short time of having nothing to show for my fire-building efforts except for blisters developing on several fingers and the invention of some creative new curses, I threw my flint and steel down the road. Even the rising sun would not warm my fingers, or anything else. Such was the curse of early spring. Yes, the snow had melted, giving the illusion that things were warmed – and

I suppose they were, with respect to winter – but the chill had gotten into me so that my joints ached and my jaw hurt from being clenched tight to keep my teeth from chattering.

With nothing else to be done, I set myself to rolling my blanket and preparing for a miserable walk back home when my new flute tumbled out from between two folds in the blanket. I remembered the night before and the power that the flute had over the fire.

Rubbing my hands together and blowing on them, I did my best to work some small amount of warmth into them. After a few moments, the stiffness in my knuckles faded. I picked up the flute, stretched my mouth wide, drew in a deep breath of that chill morning air, and played.

My fingers danced on the flute, moving faster than I had ever played any song before. Part of it was to keep them from stiffening up again and ruining the song, part of it was in frustration that I hadn't been better prepared, but most of it was knowing that the magic of this flute had burned up everything in the fire from the night before and had left no coals for me to bank for this morning. Faster and faster I played, staring at the pile of kindling and small sticks I'd built up to get my fire started. Like the night before, I played a tune I'd never played, or even heard, before. I put all my frustration and embarrassment into my music: the flush on my forehead I always got when I was foolish, and the way my ears burned when I knew I should have thought better about something.

Then, in defiance of the cold around me, I began to dance in time to the song. I was no longer some meek thing to be brought down! I was the master of my fate in all its forms. I commanded my life and my destiny. Not a season. Not a chilly morning. Me! Heir to Grandmother Elzibeth's flute and magic. I had commanded the fires the night before, completely without knowing it, but it had been my song that made them dance and revel. I would not be cold. Fire would dance again.

Smoke rose from the center of the kindling.

I played and danced harder.

Then I saw a few glowing sparks appear.

I stopped dancing.

I glared at the pile of sticks.

My song and my will were one as my fingers flew up and down, up and down.

I felt the heat growing around me as I stared, willing the sticks to light as I played. I heard the roar of flames in my ears. I smelled smoke wafting around me. Still, I only managed a few sparks.

Heat washed over me so that I was sweating underneath my cloak, but still I played on. The sticks would light. It had become a matter of pride at that point.

I drew in a quick breath of air through my nose and coughed on the smoke, interrupting my song.

In the absence of my music, a fire still roared and popped in my ears. Heat, nearly unbearable now that I no longer focused on my playing, pressed at my back. Smoke swirled around me in the morning breeze that did little to cool me.

I turned around. The heat pressing into my back struck my face like the back of my father's hand. Every house in the old village was ablaze. Black smoke billowed into the air.

For a few moments, I stood gaping as the sweat from my face poured. When I felt my eyebrows and eyelashes beginning to smolder, I snatched up my blanket and pack and hurried away, thanking all the gods and goddesses that ever were that nobody ever came here. No matter how they felt about the place, I'm sure I'd never see or hear an end to this if anyone found out I'd done it.

After a good ten minutes or so of running, I stopped and drank from my water skin. When I caught my breath and had a bit more to drink, I looked back.

A pillar of black smoke rose into the sky.

I smiled. I couldn't help it. I'd tried so hard to light a tiny fire and put so much into my song that I'd set the whole town ablaze. Then I laughed, the sound foreign to my ears, unlike any laugh I'd ever uttered before: proud, pleased, and more than a little half-crazed. I had done that. Well, I had done it with the flute, but I'd been the one playing it…the one who had channeled whatever magic lay within it and summoned a spectral dragon and then burned a village.

For a few minutes I watched the smoke rise up and billow in the high winds that carried clouds toward the distant mountains. I smiled the whole time, and sometimes, that half-mad laugh bubbled up from within me.

"I did that," I said out loud.

My grin widened.

What else could I do? I'd learned I could destroy…but…could I also create?

Pulling my attention away from the inferno I'd started, I carefully packed my things in order to have my hands free on the walk home. It was a long journey, longer if I walked slowly.

Once I had everything straightened away and slung across my shoulders and had turned back toward home, I placed the flute to my lips again.

VI

I pounded on the door several times before I heard grumbling and shuffling on the other side. The door opened and Uncle Ian blinked a few times, squinting into the fading light of dusk. Candles and a fire burned behind him. He squinted at me a moment before his eyes went wide and his mouth curved down into a frown.

"Killian?" he said.

"Good evening, Uncle Ian," I replied.

"You look…different."

I grinned. "It's my ten-and-fifth name day. I'm supposed to look different now that I'm becoming a man."

"No." He shook his head. "It's more than that. You are different. Not the same boy I spoke to at the tavern. "

"I'm not—!"

"No." He held up a finger. Leaning forward, Uncle Ian peered at my face. He stared straight into my eyes, then he looked at them from the side, first my left then my right. "It thinks it's a man, as they all do at that age…but it's not a man." He held his finger up again before I said anything. "No. Don't bother arguing. You don't understand. But something is different. Something in the eyes I've only seen in one other person."

He opened the door all the way and stood to the side. "Well…come in."

Once I entered the cottage, Uncle Ian shut the door behind me and limped over to his table. He poured a cup of tea.

"What happened?"

Rather than explain, I simply placed my flute on the table.

Uncle Ian stared at the instrument as the shadows grew even longer outside.

"Is that—?"

"Yes."

"You've played it?"

I nodded.

"And?"

I smiled. I reached for the flute, pausing just before taking hold of it.

Uncle Ian looked at me, looked at the flute, and then back at me. He licked his lips as he drew in a deep, slow breath and let it out. His eyes flicked down to the flute one more time. Then the left side of his mouth curled up into a smile, and he nodded.

I picked up the flute and played.

As I had nearly most of the way home, I played from my heart and not any song that I had known before.

The next time someone wandered even close to the direction of the old village, they would find fields and fields of lush growth, more than there should ever be this early in the spring. I'd made music of the joy of life and new beginnings. As I skipped and danced my way home to my music, the world sprang to life around me.

I began a mournful song. I played of being robbed of the prime of life by a crippling injury and the frustration of watching those who had remained home safe living full lives around him while he while giving up so much protect them. Slowly, my song changed, reversing the tune, moving back to a time when strength and vitality flowed, when weakness and pain were things of a distant, uncertain future. The song ran, jumped, danced, and fought with all the joy and vigor of the strength of a young man.

I finished my song and opened my eyes.

Uncle Ian was gone. A stranger looked back me, a young man only a few years older than I was, his hair possibly a brighter flame of red than mine.

I bolted to my feet, knocking my chair over with a crash.

"Killian!" the stranger said. "What—?" He held up his hand, and stopped.

He looked at his hand with wide-eyed curiosity, turning it again and again from the palm to the back, taking it in. He smiled, and as he did so, he lifted his fingers to his face, touching his cheeks and forehead. He chuckled a bit and stood up.

I backed away a few steps until the back of my leg came up against the chair I'd overturned.

The young man bounced on his toes, jumping slightly from side to side. A joyous laugh rumbled deep in his chest.

"Oh, Killian," the young man said, "you glorious, wonderful idiot."

"Who are you?" I asked.

"Take a look," he replied. "A very close look."

I did just that, and when I realized…my eyes grew wide as well.

"Uncle…Ian?"

"Indeed."

He danced in a circle around the table, and scooping me into a massive hug, he laughed that crazed, half-mad laugh of his. No matter how much his body might have changed, the laugh confirmed that this was Ian. I'd just meant to heal his leg. Apparently, the music had other intentions.

The embrace continued, and Ian spun me around. I grew dizzy, and it was hard to breathe. I gasped and pounded my arms against him as best I could with him squeezing me. I felt like a fish floundering about on the shore with nothing but ineffectual fins to get me back to the water.

A moment later, Ian put me down and clapped me on the shoulder.

"Sorry," he said. "Just excited."

"It's alright," I said.

Someone pounded on the door.

"Well," Ian said, as he hurried to the other room. I barely made out a muffled, "That came a bit sooner than I expected."

"What did?" I asked, following him.

He scurried back and forth across his room, between his bed, a wardrobe, and a chest, tossing clothes and odds and ends into a pack.

"Everyone else coming to figure out what's going on," He replied. "I bet your song carried further than my house."

The pounding became a banging. More voices called out, but I couldn't understand them from back here.

Ian closed up his pack and faced me.

"You need to go," he said. "Out the back. You won't be able to stay. Not after this."

He knelt down next to the bed and reached for something underneath. I heard something grate on the floor. Ian stood up, holding a sword. It wasn't the first time I'd seen one. Every year when the king's tax collector came to the village, he had two guards. Each was always armed with a sword and crossbow.

More pounding and banging sounded on the front door, accompanied by shouts and cries for Ian, wanting to know what was going on with the music.

This sword was different. Ian's sword was longer and thinner, almost as long as he was tall, with a handle so that it could be used with either one or two hands. Rather than a straight blade like the ones the guards carried, Ian's sword curved slightly along its length. The scabbard was wood, rather than leather like the ones I'd seen before. A long slit in the center of the scabbard showed the blade. Instead of the shine of metal, I saw the same dull, off-white color as my flute.

"Where did you get that?" I demanded, pointing at the weapon.

"No time to explain," Ian said, slinging the sword over his shoulder. "We have to go. Both of us. It's not going to be safe." Then he pushed his arms through the straps on the pack. Once it was on his back, it covered most of the place where the blade showed through the scabbard.

"What do you mean?" I asked. "This is home. We just explain. Think of how much I could do for everyone with this." I held up the flute.

"You think they're going to want you to use that?" Ian laughed, leaving his bedroom. "The elders remember. The last time they heard that thing, a pair of dragons came and took Grandmother Elzibeth away."

"I'll explain it to them," I said, "convince them somehow."

"You're an idiot, Killian," Ian said. "You won't get a chance to say anything." He moved to the front door and

60

lowered his voice. I could barely hear him over the shouting and pounding. "I'll leave this way. They'll be so busy wondering who I am that you'll have time to slip out the back. If you see anyone there, don't talk to them. Get to your home, get a few things for traveling as fast as you can, and leave." He lifted the latch. "Please listen to me on this, Killian. They are small-minded people, and what they cannot understand terrifies them. You will terrify them. You can only protect yourself and your family by running."

With that, Ian pulled the door open. A small crowd had gathered. I could see about a dozen people, though with the darkness falling, I suppose more might have been waiting.

"Good evening, gentles," he cried in a loud and happy voice.

The shouting died down as people stared at Ian, trying to figure out who he was and why he looked so familiar.

"Ian's coming." He started pushing his way between them. "He'll be right here. Leg hurts something fierce. Taking a while to get out of bed."

"Who are you?" Old Angus asked.

"Me?" Ian replied without stopping. "Bastard son. From the war. Came to meet my father. Met him. Unimpressed. Be on my way."

"But it's night," Old Angus called, face tightening. "Roads aren't safe."

By then, Ian had broken through the crowd and was jogging away.

"Rather risk it than spend another night around you lot," he called back.

And then he faded away into the night. Everyone who had been looking at him turned to the house. Ian had left the door open. Now they were looking at me.

A lady gasped. "He's got it."

"Put that thing down, Killian," Old Angus said, pointing his pipe stem at the flute. "Put it down before someone gets hurt."

"Might be too late," a woman said from somewhere at the back of the crowd. "I heard playing already. They were in here playing that thing."

"Settle down everyone," Old Angus said, then he looked at me and spoke as if my sense were rattled. "Now Killian, don't do anything rash."

Two younger men pushed past Old Angus, and by younger men, I mean the gray had only started showing in their beards and hair in the last few years. Tomlin and Brant, who had never had a kind word for Ian, or anyone with a drop of Elzibeth's blood in them.

"Settling down is for fools," Tomlin said. "He's played it. You can see it in his eyes. No telling what kind of hold that thing has on him."

When Tomlin and Brant got through the door, they split up so they could come at me from different directions. They glared at me, mouths clamped in thin lines. I backed away from Tomlin and Brant, trying to keep them both in my vision as I went. Two steps later, I realized that wasn't going to happen.

I really wished I'd listened to Ian, but I had been too busy trying to piece together what was going on. Well one thing I knew, I wasn't going to let them take the flute from me.

On my third step back, I bumped into the table. It startled me so much, that I jumped a little and turned around. In that moment of distraction, Tomlin and Brant came at me. Tomlin got his hand on my shoulder.

I went dead weight.

That sudden and unexpected shift pulled my shoulder out of his grasp.

When I hit the floor, I rolled under the table. More people came into the cottage. I could only think of one way out of this.

Putting the flute to my lips, I began to play a lullaby. I could put them all to sleep and escape. Tomlin and Brant flipped the table over. Something hit me hard in the shoulder.

All right, so a lullaby might not be the best thought. It took too long to get people to sleep.

Brant got hold of me this time. I stopped playing and bit his hand. He cried and let go, backing up into some of the people crowding in.

With that moment of freedom, I put the flute to my lips and played the highest, shrillest note that I could. Ian's windows shattered. People clamped their hands over their ears. My head ached with the pressure of that note filling the room. I continued the note until people's faces were scrunched in pain and discomfort. It was a challenge for me to keep my eyes open.

Once I had most of them momentarily blinded, I stopped playing and scrambled toward the bedroom.

Honestly, I've thought back on that night again and again, and even with my music, I have no possible explanation for how I made it to the bedroom and got the door closed. Maybe my small stature had some part to play. Perhaps I was more desperate to escape so they could not take the flute than they were to catch me and take the flute from me. Then again, it could be that they underestimated me. I wasn't the timid little creature I'd been when I'd left the village.

Once I got into the room, closed the door, and slammed the latch into place, my luck continued. Uncle Ian kept his wardrobe right next to the door. Standing next to the wardrobe, opposite the door, I played a deep, strong note.

The wardrobe began to shake.

Someone rattled against the door handle.

I took a deep breath and blew the note again, this time louder and deeper.

The wardrobe shook again.

Something heavy slammed against the door. At the time, I couldn't understand what this fear was born of. Looking back, I'm amazed they were so gentle with me.

I kept playing that deep note, even as the heavy something struck against the door twice more. The wardrobe shook and shook, and just as the fourth blow hit the door, splitting the wood where the latch was bolted into the wall, the wardrobe toppled over.

With what little respite that might gain, I allowed myself a few moments to recover my breath. I rubbed my temples and ran my fingers through my hair, scratching my head. This helped alleviate a bit of the headache from the high-pitched note I'd played to escape the front room.

The pounding on the door kept up, which didn't worry me any longer with the wardrobe in place. Now I just had to do something before they figured out they wouldn't break it down and someone decided to try and come through the window.

Sitting cross-legged on Uncle Ian's bed, I began to play my favorite lullaby, "Mountain Heather."

I played through the banging on the door. I played through the rapping on the window, and then through the shattering glass. I played even as my heart pounded in my chest as Master Tamsin, the candlemaker, cursed as he crawled through the broken window. I didn't speed the tempo. I didn't play any louder. Master Tamsin stood, after dropping head and shoulders first from the window and then falling awkwardly on the floor. He yawned even as he cursed again. Master Tamsin took three steps toward me and yawned again. Someone else started crawling through the window, but I couldn't tell who it was with Tamsin in the way. On his fifth step, Tamsin stopped. He blinked several times in rapid succession, tried to stifle another yawn, and took another step. On the seventh step, he slumped forward, asleep. The person partway through the window was also asleep. The pounding on the bedroom door had stopped.

Still, even though it seemed that I was safe, I kept playing. I played through the song twice more, just to be sure. When I finished, I lowered the flute to my lap and listened.

Nothing.

Well, nothing except the soft snores coming from the man trapped in the window.

I didn't have to think too long, all of about ten heartbeats if that, to decide I needed to follow Uncle Ian's example and leave the village. If this was the reaction I was going to get without the townsfolk having seen me actually do anything with the magic, I didn't want to imagine what they would do once they woke up.

Since I didn't know how long they would stay asleep, haste was at the front of my mind. The problem was, I'd trapped myself in this room. I could have tried moving the wardrobe the same way I'd put it there, but I didn't want to risk playing anything else for fear of waking them.

So, I went over to the man in the window. It was one of my older cousins, Dannil. I grabbed the back of his coat and pulled. Now, Dannil was only six years older than I was, and he wasn't an overly large young man, that coupled with saying I was a scrawny thing would have been a compliment. I struggled to pull him out of the window. By the time he finally slid out and crumpled onto the floor, I'd ripped his coat and trousers, given him a nasty gash on the leg from a piece of glass still stuck in the window pane, and his arm made a sickening snap when he landed on it.

I froze for a moment, not even breathing, waiting for Dannil to wake up. He didn't. He only gave a pitiful whimper and then went back to snoring.

"Sorry," I said.

Then I crawled out of the window.

The crowd of people that had gathered around Uncle Ian's house lay asleep in the yard. Everyone I saw was asleep as I went to my parents' home. They looked as peaceful as babes, which shouldn't have surprised me.

When I reached my parents' house, Mother was asleep with her head on the table. Dishes had been set out for the meal. Stew bubbled in the cooking pot. I couldn't find Father. I hadn't seen him in the mob outside Uncle Ian's, and I wanted to believe that he hadn't joined them.

My recent adventure in the old village taught me a lot about what I'd need for a life on the run. My pack was still next to the table in Uncle Ian's cottage, so I took Father's. I filled it with several changes of clothes, an extra blanket, a few of Mother's needles and a spool of thread, bread, cheese, the last of the winter store of dried fruit, and a good knife. I also took Father's warmest cloak for the same reason I'd taken his pack, and I rolled my last two blankets up and tied them to the pack.

Once I had everything I thought I needed, I slung the pack onto my shoulders and headed for the door out of the kitchen. Then I stopped. I looked at my mother, sleeping peacefully, and considered what the town might do to my family. Considering how they'd treated me just because I reminded them a little of Grandmother Elzibeth, they might do something foolish to retaliate against my parents after what I'd done tonight.

Hoping that it would be enough to make people think that my parents were also victims of whatever wickedness the townsfolk thought I held in my heart, I set about making a mess in the kitchen, front room, and in my parents' room. I went over to the fireplace and scattered the wood all around, even threw one of the logs through a window. I bit my lip and pulled my hair when I heard the shattering glass. Even my muttered apologies didn't ease the cold and sinking sensation just behind my naval. It wasn't anything compared to the loathing I felt when I moved the loose stone in the corner and took out the coin purse I knew my father kept hidden there. My hope was that if it looked like I had robbed my parents, the village wouldn't turn on them because they couldn't find me.

When I got to the door again, the purse weighed so heavy in my hand that I couldn't walk out of the door with it. I thought for a moment, looked around, and came up with a plan. I put a chair on the table, climbed up, and pushed the money bag deep into the thatching of the roof. It might be months or years before Father looked there while repairing the roof, but he should eventually find it.

Conscience eased a bit, I climbed down, kissed my mother on the cheek, and left.

I'd considered trying to find my father, to see if he was part of the mob that had come for me and Uncle Ian, but I decided against it.

To this day, I choose to believe he wasn't.

VII

I traveled as quickly as I could, taking as little rest as possible. The first few hours of the first night, I only thought to put as much distance between myself and the village as I could. I hoped the people there would sleep through the night and upon waking suffer some confusion as they tried to figure out what had happened. Even if they did wake before sunrise, I didn't expect that they would begin chasing me until dawn.

As hours passed, I slowed my pace. Now that I had a decent head start, or so I hoped, I could set a steady pace that I could maintain for hours. This would serve me better than moving faster now, and thus, tiring much sooner. The slower and steadier pace also gave me a chance to think. I've met people who thrive when in the midst of frantic and high-tension situations, even going so far as to make choices that serve as a catalyst to create an environment where they feel they can thrive. I am not one of them. When I notice these people doing these things, I can't help but wonder how they don't collapse from exhaustion. Slowing my stride allowed me to relax and consider what I should do next, beyond getting as far from my home as possible

The story would spread. As the night grew colder, I imagined the people of my former home – I had no illusions that I'd ever return there – scattering to all the neighboring towns and villages to warn them about the terror that I'd become. After those first few villages and towns, the tale would spread on the wind. For the moment, I was ahead of it, but soon – within a few days at most, and that's only if I was very, very lucky – the tale would spread beyond me and grow with the telling. Within weeks – again, if I was very, very lucky – everyone would be seeking the young man with the flaming red hair who consorted with demons and drew upon their dark powers to cause people to sleep away years of their lives. That, I could not outrun…but, maybe, just maybe, with the help of a certain magic flute, I might be able to outsmart it…maybe.

A few hours later, I stood atop a hill looking down on the nearest village to my home. The moon hung low in the sky, and the sun wasn't showing even the tiniest bit of glow in the eastern sky. I'd walked around the entire village so that the wind was at my back and blowing toward my destination. Better to carry my song down there. I placed my flute to my lips and began to play a song to help my mission. Acceptance, belief, pity, and concern wafted on the breeze to the town.

As the sun rose the next morning, I sat on the steps of the inn the next village over. I heard the door open behind me.

"Oh," a man's voice said. "Good morning. May I help you?"

I can only imagine what I looked like, my small frame hunched over, huddled in Father's cloak, bedroll on my knees. When I stood up and turned around, Master Tols, the innkeeper, looked down on me from the wide porch. His mouth dropped, which made his jowls quiver. His deep brown eyes grew wide, looking like over-fried eggs. I lowered my hood and gave him a tentative and timid smile.

"Young Killian?" Master Tols asked.

I'm sure he only recognized me by my size and shock of red hair. Dirt covered my face. Tears, now dried, had streaked through the dirt, though my nose still ran. I'd passed through a patch of onions on the way here.

"Good morning," I said, wiping my nose with the back of my sleeve.

"What are you doing here?" Tols asked.

"Everything is crazy back home," I replied. "Some man came to visit my Uncle Ian…"

"Daft Ian?" Tols asked.

I nodded.

"Never would have thought anyone would come to visit him, but go on."

"He was a young man, with a strange sword," I said. "I saw it. The sword, that is. It didn't look like metal. The blade was some whitish color." Tols took a step back, covering his mouth with his hand. I'd guessed right. "Have you ever heard of such a thing?"

He nodded. "Things from back in the war. Terrible business, those blades."

Those? More than one? Did anyone else from my home know that Ian had one? Is that why he was the other outcast?

"But go on."

"Well," I said. "Most of it is..." I licked my lips, blinked my eyes, and wobbled a bit on my feet.

"Oh, my dear Killian," Tols said. "Where are my manners? Come in. Come in. You must have been walking all night. Let's get some tea in you and some breakfast."

He ushered me into the inn, and in just a short while, I sat at the bar with a mug of tea with a dab of honey and a fresh-out-of-the-oven berry muffin right in front of me. While I wanted nothing more than to devour the muffin, I could not. It wouldn't serve my plan at all. Instead, I nibbled on it while drinking the tea.

"Well this man with the sword," I said between bites of the muffin and yawns. "I saw him go to Uncle Ian's house."

"Now Killian," Tols said. "The only thing I want to know is, are you hurt?"

"No, sir," I said, putting another tiny morsel of the muffin into my mouth. "Not really. It got crazy for a while. Some people thought I was behind the sleeping, because I'm like my Grandmother Elzibeth." I yawned. "Have you heard of her?"

"The one that supposedly got carried away by dragons?" Tols asked.

I nodded, stifling another yawn with the back of my hand while rubbing my eye with my other hand. At this point, the yawning and eye rubbing wasn't an act any more. Even though I was young, I'd walked more in the last two days than I had in the last three weeks combined, and hadn't had any decent rest since before my fifth-and-ten.

I remember taking a sip of my tea and then Master Tols helping me into a room with a cot, then I was lying down and he was putting a blanket over me.

"You rest a bit, young Killian," Tols said. "We'll hear your story after."

Despite my efforts to stay awake – I didn't have time to sleep; I needed to tell my story and be on to the next town – sleep overcame me. Dreams of music and dragons and flames warred in my mind as I tossed and turned on the cot. Between the cot being uncomfortable and the frantic dreams plaguing me, I couldn't reach truly restful sleep. Hours later, after a dream where dragon fire had burned my flute in my hands, killing my music forever, I sat bolt upright.

The sun shone in through a sliver of space between the curtains. When Master Tols had put me to bed, the light through that crack had been the muted hazy light of dawn. Now it was a bright beam through the dim room. I'd slept until sometime midday. This did not help my plan in the least.

I leapt from the bed and gathered my things. I'd have to make my story to Master Tols very short if I wanted to make it to the next town with enough time to tell my next story at their tavern. I left the room, rushed into the common room…and stopped.

People filled the room. It seemed at least half the village sat looking at me. I stood looking back, feeling the weight of all those eyes on me.

"Aaahhh," I said after a moment, wanting to fill the silence with something. "Good afternoon."

Master Tols came to my side and guided me to a chair by the hearth. The chair was set in the spot reserved for minstrels and entertainers. My mind flashed to the flute tucked away deep in my bedroll. My fingers itched with how much I wanted to take the flute out and play for these people. But I couldn't. To do so would likely destroy the careful plan I'd come up with the previous night. As it was, my hours of fitful sleep hadn't helped my plan at all.

"Now," Master Tols said. "Tell us what happened."

76

"Well," I said. "I told you about the young man with the strange sword." Master Tols and several others nodded. Of course he would have told them that much. "Well, I was coming back from an adventure my father let me go on for my ten-and-fifth name day." I added that detail on the spur of the moment. It wouldn't do my story well to leave that part out and have other people tell them where I'd gone. "I went to the Old Village, as my people call it. Some of us go there, to prove our courage."

"Did you find anything while you were there?" a man in the back of the crowd asked. I couldn't make him out in the shadows back there with all the other people in the way.

"No, sir," I replied. "Unless you count the cold and stiff back I got sleeping on the ground. On my truth, it wasn't much of an adventure."

That got a few laughs from the crowd.

"When I finally got home. I saw the man go to Uncle Ian's house. I saw the sword. Having just come from my adventure, my blood was high and I wanted to know more about it. So, I went to Uncle Ian's house. The man was pleasant enough. When he heard that I play the flute, he asked me to play a song for him. I did. He asked me to play another. Minding my manners, I did. In the middle of that song, he pulled the sword and started dancing around the cottage, almost as if he were fighting imaginary opponents. Before my song was over, someone pounded on the door. I stopped playing, but the man with the strange sword kept dancing that strange dance. The door crashed open. People rushed in. The man kept dancing. Several people fell asleep right there in Ian's front room. Several attacked the man. As he escaped, he beat them down with his hands and elbows and knees and the butt of his sword. Then they came after me and Uncle Ian. Master Tomlin was screaming that I'd cursed them with my music. I think the only reason I managed to get away is because everyone was falling asleep around me. I don't know what happened to Uncle Ian, but I got to my house and got my things and ran. I made it a little out of the village before I fell down. I woke up in the middle of the night and started running. I don't know what I'm going to do, but I can't go back there. I saw it in his eyes; Master Tomlin meant to kill me."

"Don't fret any over it, young Killian," Master Tols said. "You've always been a joy to have the times you've come for gatherings. We can find some work for you here, settle you down, keep you safe. I know a story or two about those swords from when I fought in the king's army. Anyone comes looking to cause you trouble, we'll set them straight."

Many of the people there, especially the older ones I knew who had daughters, nodded along with Master Tols's words. I'd been expecting that.

"Thank you," I said, "But I couldn't possibly expect you to take on my troubles. You know how things like this spread. Soon, it won't just be my village. Word is going to spread, and I won't have anywhere safe to go within a week's…no…a month's journey from my home. I need to try and stay ahead of it."

"True lad," an older woman said. "That word will spread."

"We could keep him safe," someone said from my right.

"No," another voice came from the back of the crowd. "He may be a good lad. I've no doubt of that. But trouble like this is something we don't need. Killian has the right of it. Best we can do is make sure he's safe and well-provisioned for his journey."

"Mayor Brantson has the truth of it," Tols said. "We can also share Killian's story to any who pass through. Sure enough his people got their own story to tell, and who knows how terrible it will be. Killian, you come over to the bar, and I'll serve you up something good. Everyone else, be back about your business. If you have anything to spare for poor Killian, bring it by and we'll see he gets it."

And so it was, about an hour later I walked out of the village, pack twice as heavy as it had been when Master Tols had taken me in that morning. Even still, my step was light and I felt ready to make it to the next town before too late.

"Hold there a moment," a man called behind me.

I stopped and turned around. An older man in clothes slightly finer than those of the rest of the townsfolk approached me. He had a long staff in one hand, and used it as a walking stick. Though older than most men I knew, Mayor Brantson still carried himself straight, tall, and fit from tending his sheep and cattle.

"Mayor," I said, as he came up to me. "Thank you for everything."

"You're welcome," the Mayor said. "I wanted to let you know before you leave that you should not be too proud of yourself and to be careful. This morning, when I woke and went to tend my flock and herd, I found a note pinned to my door with a knife I'd given an old friend back when we were young, foolish, and our heads swam with glories. Much like you."

Mayor Brantson fished in his pocket with his free hand. He brought out a folded piece of paper and handed it to me. I took it, unfolded it, and read it.

"Dane. The troubles may be starting again. Watch over your people. A young man with a knack for music may come needing help. Aid him how you can. He has no fault besides his blood and how it sings to him. I'm back to my old life. The life I wanted. Keep your staff and knife close. Watch your people. I will send word of news as I can. – Ian."

I refolded the paper and handed it back to the mayor.

"What do you mean to do?" I asked.

"To you?" he replied. "Nothing. Be about your way. And if what I suspect is true, I only ask that you go far, far away from all of us. I just want to know, what did you do for your parents before you fled?"

I looked at my feet and chewed my lip. I'd been caught, at least partially. I could try and lie my way through this, but something told me the truth would be better.

"I made it look like I robbed them," I said. "I hoped that would keep the people at home from turning on them."

"Not a bad plan, and it might work," Mayor Brantson said. "I've sent some of my biggest and strongest lads to fetch them and bring them here, just to be safe."

"Do you have someone with a fast horse who could catch them with a message?" I asked. "I hid a purse of money up in the thatching. I thought it might the other people in the village might not be so quick to judge my parents if they thought I'd robbed them. That will help them start their new life here,"

He nodded. "I'll see it done."

"Thank you," I said.

"One last thing." His voice grew low and hard. "Take care with that flute if you have it. Those of us who fought in the King's War remember, and some of us have ways around what you can do.

"You fought with Uncle Ian," I said.

He nodded. "And helped carry him home." He fixed me with an unblinking stare. "You are stepping into a dangerous, dangerous game, Killian. Take each step on your journey with care."

I took his words in, and nodded. With nothing else to say, I turned again and began my journey to the next town. My step was not nearly as light as it had been before Mayor Brantson had stopped me.

VIII

Two months later, I stood on a table next to the hearth of a tavern, in a town large enough to have three such taverns and two inns. I played the bone-white flute with abandon. The patrons clapped along in time and laughed as eight chairs danced around the center of the room. People sitting in the chairs held on with all their strength, or at least all the strength they had considering how drunk they were. It was a grand game. Whoever could hold on the longest wouldn't have to pay his or her debt at the end of the evening.

I could recount my travels before that evening in detail, chronicling every word of every conversation I had, and all the aches and pains I suffered on the road. However, to do so would make this portion of my tale overly long. Please indulge my brevity as I explain how it was that I found myself, not just playing in a tavern, but also having people accept and enjoy my strange magic.

For a fortnight after the incident at my village, I made my way doing odd jobs, any work I could find for a meal, a bed, or corner of a stable for a night, or if I was really lucky, a small bit of coin. I also told wild tales about that night back in my village to explain why I was on the road. The further I got from home, the wilder, madder, and crazier the tales grew. I got a cap to hide my hair, so sometimes I could tell the tale from the side of the townsfolk, making the story seem legendary. Most times when I told this, I assumed the name Frances and spoke of finding my cousin who was always the victim of circumstances far beyond his control. These stories I usually told to people I passed on the road, asking if they'd seen him. Then, for the next two weeks, I spread stories of the minstrel with the magic flute, that made chairs dance, put children to sleep with no fuss, and made village and town bullies fall in love with the livestock for a night; even fire and smoke would perform at the command of his flute. During this time, I kept the hat firmly on my head and made sure to keep my face darkened, especially my eyebrows, so I when I spoke of this minstrel's red hair, I would not be associated with him. Everywhere I went, and everyone I met, I asked if they had met such a person, for I wanted to see him firsthand to see if the wild claims were true.

Then, having saved enough coin and collected enough food to last me a good while, I made my way into some forested hills to practice on my flute. I learned how to manipulate fire and smoke first, as that's what I'd had the most problems with – it wouldn't do to burn down a tavern where I was trying to play. I managed to not burn the forest to the ground, though twice it was a near thing. After I got that under control, I began to increase my experimentation. Soon, plants came alive with movement depending on the tunes I played, rocks rolled uphill at my direction, and within a fortnight of my first entering the woods, the animals themselves followed the whims of my music.

When I reached a level of skill and understanding of the flute where my intention, the music, and the effect combined in perfect unison, I resumed my travels for a few days, continuing to spread stories of the magic minstrel. When the legend I created had grown to the point I heard about him without beginning the conversation, I knew it was time. In between two towns, I washed the grime from my face and tucked my hat away, showing off my flaming red hair.

The next town I came to, a little girl ran up to me and asked, "Are you the magic minstrel?"

I smiled. "What do you think?"

"I think you are!" she cried. "You have the hair and stand the right height. Will you make my house dance? I heard you once made two towns change places."

I laughed. It seemed my legend had grown a little in my absence, as stories are wont to do. But before I confirmed who I was, I had to test something.

"I hadn't heard that particular tale," I said. "But I did hear that he put a village to sleep for a hundred years for attacking him."

"I don't believe that," she said. "That's too long. Maybe a few days, just to teach them a lesson. But who would be silly enough to attack someone so wonderful?"

"Who indeed?" I said, sliding my flute out from underneath my cloak and tapping myself on the chest as I added, "Certainly not I."

Her face stretched as her eyes widened. She might have smiled in joy and wonder, if her mouth hadn't opened as wide as it possibly could have gone. She pointed at the flute, shook in place, and then looked around frantically for someone, anyone to share this news with. She tried to shout at some other children playing further up the street, but only managed a single shrill squeak of excitement.

I cleared my throat. The little girl turned back to me. Her face relaxed enough so that now she was actually smiling, and nodding eagerly.

"Would you care to show me to the tavern?" I asked. "And I'll speak to someone about playing this evening."

"Yes!" she said, and started off. "This way!"

She set such a pace that I had to jog to keep up with her.

And that evening gave birth to the legend of the magic minstrel. He would appear at the edge of whatever town he had decided to play for that night, reveal himself to a child or group of children, and have them escort him to the town inn or tavern. Stories live and breathe and gain immortality through the excitement of children, and few forces in the world match the stories that ignite children's imaginations into a conflagration of wonder. By the time the magic minstrel began to make appearances, two stories had spread about the young man with the flaming red hair and a magic flute. One about how this vile trickster cursed people with injuries in their sleep, and one about a joyous trickster who made furniture dance, flames and smoke tell stories in the air, and many other wonders. One story moved slowly. The other spread like unto pollen on the wind, so that in places where the two stories met…one usually ground the other to silence beneath the wave of wonder it rode upon.

And so it came to pass that I stood on a table next to the hearth, making chairs dance and people laugh, when the door opened, swinging wide and banging into the wall. The window closest to the door rattled in its frame. A few ladies and children shrieked, and one man close to the door sprayed his drink in surprise. My song died. The chairs clattered together in a heap.

Ian stood in the doorway. It took me a moment to recognize him. He wore the red and blue livery of those who served the crown. That odd sword poked up over his left shoulder. His eyes swept across the room, and when his gaze fell on me, he stood glaring at me. Silence hung in the tavern, the pop and snap of burning logs the only sound, and each one sounding almost like thunder. After a few moments, when I said nothing, he arched his eyebrow at me.

"Uhhh…" I said. "I'll…uuuummm…play again in a bit. Tavern master, a drink for my friend. I haven't seen him in months. We…uh…have some catching up to do."

I waved Ian over. I couldn't think of him as Daft Uncle Ian, or even Uncle Ian, as I watched him walk through the tavern. This was a man I could believe injured his leg in a war. His eyes did not stay fixed on any point for more than a few heartbeats while he walked toward me. He'd see something, his eyes would move up and down, examining whatever had drawn his attention, and then his gaze would be moving again.

I'd gotten fairly good at reading the subtle parts of people's expressions. Sometimes, though few and rare these times were, the magic minstrel was not well received. Seeing danger before I got too close had become a handy skill.

When Ian reached halfway across the room, two more men in blue and red livery came through the door and stepped to either side. I considered this might be a good time to scamper out the back. The room was crowded enough that Ian had to weave through the people as he walked toward me. I could probably make it to the kitchen and away, but as if my thoughts betrayed me, I heard a cry of surprise from the kitchen and another man in red and blue came through from the back, blocking my way.

Patrons of the tavern began to whisper. This situation was going to get out of hand, and I shuddered to think of what it might do to the reputation I'd carefully crafted for the magic minstrel. Still, it wasn't as bad as all that. I could salvage this. True, Ian was sharper and a lot less daft than I remember. True, he'd surprised me and had thought of my possible escapes before I had. That didn't mean he had the complete upper hand. I had something he didn't, and I'd gotten a lot better with it since the last time we'd seen each other.

"Don't," Ian said, even as I began to lift the flute to my lips.

He didn't raise his voice, but something about his tone struck me deep to the core. This was the same man who had convinced me to defy my father and wander up to the old village. He had convinced me without me actually realizing that he was the one who had done the convincing – though in hindsight, it's not too challenging a task to convince boys that age that setting out on a grand adventure is completely and wholly their idea.

His voice carried the same aura of command, only now he spoke with the conviction of a man who expected to be obeyed, and it lacked any of the subtlety he'd had months before.

I climbed down from my table and sat down.

Ian sat across from me.

The tavern master brought two mugs and a pitcher.

"Sir," the tavern master said, his voice full of the same respect and deference his body showed by bobbing up and down in silly bowing movements as he spoke each word, "we are all loyal subjects here, and wish no trouble or harm upon His Majesty, His Majesty's family, or those who wear His Majesty's livery."

"I will speak your words to His Majesty," Ian said, "just as you have spoken them to me, the next time I see His Majesty."

Somehow I doubted Ian's ability to adopt the faint edge of terror in the man's voice. Now, it's not that the king ruled by fear in those days. The king had only sat upon the throne a few short years since his father had passed – may the king live forever – and so was still coming into his own as a monarch, especially having come into his throne much later than expected. His father had lived longer than anyone had anticipated, long enough so that his son, the new king, had children of his own, three daughters. The new king seemed to rule fairly, and no troubles had arisen with him assuming the throne – very much unlike what had happened when his father had taken the throne in Ian's youth.

Ian took a drink from his mug. He nodded.

"Highhill Dark," he said. "Developed a taste for it."

"I felt it appropriate," I replied, "as this brew stands at the center of how I came to this place in my life." I took a drink. "I never got a chance to thank you."

"Do not thank me quite yet," Ian said. "A man hears things as he wanders about the kingdom. People tell stories. The more wondrous the stories, the more often people tell them. For example, it's a challenge to pass through any place where a dozen or so people gather without hearing some tidbit about this enigmatic magical minstrel with his legendary flute the color of bone. I love hearing those tales. Do you know why? Of course you don't. I love hearing those tales because I know the truth of them, and I know of my part in the making of them. Grand stories, those. Warms my heart every time I hear them. Then there are other tales that one hears, though less frequently than those of the magic minstrel. These tales are not the same joyous, happy tales, rather they are a bit more sinister. These tales speak of a strange man who wanders about the countryside with a stranger sword…a sword the color of bone. Tales of this man and his sword, rather than an impetuous youth with a magic flute, traveling about causing mischief at best – such as the story that speaks of him placing a strange slumber upon certain village for three days and nights – and, well…I'll leave off telling of this man's other exploits, for they are dark and grim indeed, and this is a pleasant evening."

My mouth suddenly went dry. I took a long drink of Highhill Dark.

Perhaps one of the major reasons that the magic minstrel tales defeated the terrible bringer of sleep tales is because someone had also spread stories about a strange man, also with red hair, who did a strange, mystic, and hypnotic dance with a sword the color of bone that put anyone who viewed this dance into a deep, unnatural slumber. Those stories might have then made people discount the terrible bringer of sleep stories a little faster, because no one – at least no one that I knew of – told tales of a strange man with a strange sword doing anything good. So, many people believed that those telling the tales of the terrible bringer of sleep were just getting confused. And well…I might have had some small hand in helping more than a few towns and villages come to the conclusion that people were confusing those two stories.

"That," I said. "Well…I…"

"Save it," Ian said. "Your reluctance to speak says enough. At least you have the good sense to be scared now. You should have considered that before spreading the tales, considering how they treated you at home based only on the tales of Grandmother Elzibeth. You're a young man, Killian. You already have a legend greater than most men dream of in a lifetime. Tales that hang about a man can be dangerous, dangerous things. Don't bother arguing. Even tales that make a man seem great and wonderful can be a danger. Sometimes those are the tales that pose the greatest threat to a man."

"How?" I asked.

"Those tales are the ones that get you noticed," Ian said, sweeping his hand across the crowd gathered in the tavern. "Think of all the people that have noticed you. Think of all the others who have heard of you. Someday you might wish to be nothing more than a young man in a village that no one has ever heard of."

"I doubt that," I said, and jingled the coins in the purse on my belt.

"Of course," Ian said. "And I'm sure that you won't see any danger in my purpose here."

I shrugged. "What is your purpose here?"

"Word of you has gotten back to the king and his daughters." Ian took a long drink from his mug. "They want you to come and perform at the palace. Once I heard that, I volunteered to fetch you myself."

I grinned. I was to play for the king! I immediately began to consider what sort of songs I would play for the royal family and what riches he would bestow upon me.

I stopped grinning when Ian reached across the table and slapped the side of my head.

"Stop that," Ian snarled. "This is not about your daydreams. This is about the king determining what manner of threat you might be."

"What? A threat? Me?"

"You think it's silly? You can't imagine that someone might be scared of you?"

"Well…I suppose I can understand that common village folk might have cause to fear me. But a king? I don't see how. I mean… Really? But, he's a king?"

"And you think a king cannot know fear?" Ian asked. "Or do you think a king need not fear the same thing the common man fears?"

"That," I replied. "Why should a king fear the concerns of the common man?"

"First." Ian leaned forward. "The king rules an entire country of common men. He is charged with their safety and prosperity. If his subjects fear a thing, the wise king will always take notice.

"Second." Ian leaned closer. "If I were a king, and I heard tales of a young man with a flute that could put whole villages to sleep, command fire to dance, and bring mundane objects to life, I should very much like to know more about this man. For a king must ask himself, what would make such a man turn this power from amusing the common folk to tormenting the common folk? What would make this man turn this power against me?"

"Oh," I said. "Oh."

I took a long drink. And then another.

"So," Ian said. "We will enjoy the rest of the evening. Play for the people. Drink. Be Merry. Bask in their adoration." He drained his drink in three great gulps and slammed the mug on the table, startling a few people nearby. "Tomorrow we will begin our journey toward the capital, and you will not play again until you play before the king."

Ian stood up and started away.

I went to work finishing my Highhill Dark.

"Oh, Killian," Ian said.

I looked up from my drink. He'd only taken two steps, and now he looked down on me, looming with the lamps and candles behind him. With his face shrouded in shadows, Ian cut a terrifying figure.

"Don't think to try and run. I'm older, craftier, and smarter than you. If you run, I will find you again, and when I do, I'll take the flute from you and escort you to His Majesty in chains on the back of my horse."

I nodded. I had no reason to doubt him.

Ian and the other soldiers left.

A short while later, I resumed playing and entertaining. Try as I might, I could not achieve the same energy I had before my uncle had found me. I tried to picture him in my mind as Daft Uncle Ian again, to take some of my fear away. I could not. While I recognized the way he spoke, and the resemblance he had to the image of Daft Uncle Ian in my memory, this man was not the same man I'd healed a few months before. This Ian was a man who had been strong and had that strength ripped from him in his prime, and then he'd had that strength returned. I did not doubt a single word he spoke.

I was going to see the king, and as the evening went on, I grew less and less eager for that particular performance.

IX

"Don't," Ian said.

"Don't what?" I asked, doing my best to play innocent.

"I saw that longing look over toward that tavern," Ian said, "and your shuffling feet. You might as well have jumped up and down and pleaded, 'Uncle Ian, can I please, please, please go and play my flute for the people. Just one song, and I promise that I won't use the flute to make any magic. Really!' So...to answer your question...don't ask. And keep your hair tucked into your hat."

"You forgot, 'I'll be your best friend,' sir," Connar, one of the guardsmen, added as the other three guardsmen laughed.

They didn't even have the decency to try and stifle their laughter by turning away or pretending to cough. I'd been the butt of everyone's jokes and japes and jibes ever since we left the tavern where they had found me.

I crossed my arms and did my best not to pout. I definitely did not look longingly at the tavern across the street from the general store. Well, not for more than a heartbeat or two.

"I just wanted a drink and a decent meal," I said. "Is that so bad?"

"It is if someone recognizes you," Ian replied. "His Majesty was quite specific with his command. You were not to use the magic of that flute or play for another audience until after you play for him."

I turned to face him. "Well how could I, with the course you've set us?"

Two weeks we'd been traveling, and not once had we stopped in any town. We slept on the cold earth, eating cold cheese, hard bread, and dried meat more often than not. Ian even kept our fires small on the rare evenings that he allowed them. This was the first time we'd approached anything more than a solitary farmhouse, because we'd run out of every last bit of food.

"That's exactly why," Ian responded. "Connar and Alynn, you see to resupplying us." Ian tossed Connar a small bag of coins. "Rolf and Pyrce, with me and our guest. We will be about finding a custom house."

"A custom house?" My voice did not crack, and I was not shrieking. "This town has at least two fine inns."

"Custom house," Ian repeated. "Best we not take you where you'll be tempted. Let's be about it, gentlemen. The sooner we get to bed, the sooner we will rise, and the sooner we can be back on the road."

With that, Ian started down the street at a brisk pace.

Groaning, I followed. The morning after he'd found me, Ian showed me the manacles and chains he'd brought to make good on his promise if I tried to run. Not for the first time, I found myself silently cursing myself for giving Mad Uncle Ian his health and youth back. Yes, in the past two weeks, I'd managed to think of Ian as my uncle again, mostly because he had treated me like a petulant child, and I'd replaced "daft" with "mad" as a prefix to his name because he was so bloody quick to anger and suspect me of wrongdoing. Not that I'd been tempted to play now and then, but I wasn't about to risk those chains; however, Mad Uncle Ian wouldn't even allow me to play my ordinary wooden flute.

We found the custom house with little difficulty. It was just down the way from the inns and taverns. The place had once been a fine house, having belonged to a woman widowed in the war Ian had fought in during his first youth. She'd never bothered to remarry, and so had turned the house into a custom house to keep the place. She and Ian haggled for the better part of an hour. He managed to get one of the private rooms with twin double bunks and one bed. Five places for men to sleep. No need to guess who would be sleeping on the floor.

A short while later, I lay in the corner on my unrolled bedding as we waited for Connar and Alynn to return. Rolf and Pyrce were playing cards between the bunks. I could hear the chime of coins from Uncle Ian's bed.

"Hopefully it's a good night for Alynn," Ian said. "Our coin is spreading thin, and we have a good ways yet to go."

"He seemed to have that gleam in his eye, sir," Pyrce said.

"He'll be back before we know it with half the town bagged up, sir," Rolf said. "Good thing you sent Connar with him to help carry it all back. Pyrce would have made a botch of it."

"Hey!" Pyrce said, tossing down a card. They ribbed him about being a bit shorter than the rest of them, though he towered a full head taller than me "I can carry a load just as well as any of you."

"If we need money," I started...

"No," Uncle Ian said.

"I don't have to..."

"No," Uncle Ian said.

"But..."

"No," all three of them said together, and then laughed.

"Fine," I muttered. "Just trying to help."

"You were trying to do or say anything you can to get in front of a group of people and play," Uncle Ian said.

Rolling over to face the wall, I pulled the blankets over my head. This wasn't the first time I'd bitten the inside of my cheek to keep from muttering "ingrate" or some even less polite terms toward my Uncle. I tried to block out

Pyrce and Rolf bantering back and forth and the clink of Ian's coins.

I'd almost managed to steady my breathing and find a relatively comfortable position when the door banged open. The noise startled me so that I spun around, reaching to my belt for the flute that wasn't there.

Pyrce cursed.

Rolf tripped over his chair as he tried to get up, spin, and draw his weapon at the same time.

Connar hurried into the room, Alynn right behind him. Connar stepped over Rolf and handed a sheaf of parchment to Uncle Ian. It had writing scrawled across one side. In the dim candlelight, I could only make out one word, REWARD, before Ian flipped it over. His face seemed to grow harder and tighter with each word he read. He muttered something under his breath that I couldn't make out. Connar, who stood closest to him, stepped back two paces.

"Sir?" Rolf said, getting to his feet. "What is it?"

Ian handed Rolf the parchment. He and Pyrce read it together. Pyrce's mouth opened wider and wider as he read.

"Can this be real?" Rolf said. "Including that reward?"

"You never mind the reward," Ian said. "We are king's men, and we serve the king and his family with our lives for the honor of doing so. Not for some reward, especially not this."

"We are going to do something?" Connar said.

"I don't know," Ian said. "I have to think. I'll be back."

With that, he strapped his sword to his back and left the room.

"What is that about?" I asked, pointing to the parchment.

"Never you mind what it is," Rolf said. "The captain will let you know what it's about if he thinks you need to know."

"Fine," I said.

I lay down again, pulled the covers over my head again…but this time, I did not try to push them out of my mind. I listened. I'd grown accustomed to listening to them without seeming to. As much as I played the part of going along with this, I was always on the lookout for some chance to get away. Well, with Mad Uncle Ian having taken my flute, such a chance seemed rare. Until tonight. He'd gone out and left his pack behind. My flute was in that pack.

"What do we do about this?" Alynn asked.

"We do what the captain says we do," Connar said. "As we always do. No more. No less."

"But…" Alynn started.

"No buts," Connar interrupted. "That's the way of it. Best accept it."

After a slight pause, Rolf said, "No, lad. Don't bother with the arguing or debating. You're not a regular soldier any longer."

I imagined Alynn opening his mouth to continue to protest before Rolf cut him off. I'd seen it over and over as we traveled. Something would be as Alynn wasn't used to, and one of the other three would stop him and explain as Rolf did now with, "Remember lad, you're not a standard soldier any more. You are training for one of the blades. That means different rules. Captain has to decide which task the king thinks is our greater duty."

"It's obvious which…"

"No it's not," Connar said. "You've got a lot to learn about the way a king must think, and that's why you got assigned to the captain. So, do yourself a kindness. Close your mouth, listen, watch, learn. Then, when the captain finally asks you a question, you'll know you're beginning to start thinking of answers for yourself."

"Pyrce?" Alynn almost sounded like he was pleading for the shorter man to take his side in this.

"Oh, no," Pyrce said. "They have the right of it. It wasn't that long ago I was in your place. I'm still waiting for the captain to ask my opinion on something, but I have served under him long enough to know that while this may look like a simple choice, it's not. Not even close. I will give some advice in this. Get some sleep. One way or the other, no matter what the captain decides, tomorrow will be a long, hard day of traveling."

"Fine," Alynn said.

A moment later, I heard bedding rustling in one of the bunks.

This might be my chance.

I got up with one of my blankets and went over to Ian's bed.

"And just what do you think you're doing?" Rolf asked.

"I'm going to lie on this bed that no one is using," I said. "Ian won't be back for several hours. When he does get back, I'll move back to the floor. But until then, I'm not about to let this bed go to waste."

Rolf and Connar looked at each other.

I reached into my purse and drew out four silver marks.

"Before we argue about rank and preference," I said. "I'll buy the privilege of sleeping in this bed, even if it is just for a few hours."

Connar shrugged. "A silver mark is a silver mark, and the captain's probably going to be a while. I don't have issue with this if you lads don't."

"Fine," Rolf said. "Let's all get some rest."

I handed out the silver marks all around. Keeping my mouth from splitting into a wide grin might have been the hardest thing I've ever had to do. The thought that this was only the first stage of my plan of escape and that things could still go terribly wrong if I gave myself away kept my emotions reigned in.

I lay down on the bunk, my feet pointing toward the foot of the bed where Ian had laid his pack. Stretching out, I kicked it off the bed. The contents at the top, Ian's extra shirts and stockings, spilled out.

"You'll likely pay for that later," Pyrce said.

"Perhaps," I said. "But for now, it's worth it."

I stretched out underneath my blanket.

Once Alynn and Pyrce had climbed up into their bunks, Rolf blew out the candle, plunging the room into near darkness.

As I lay staring up into nothing, I worried a bit about falling asleep, but I was so excited about the thought of escaping that sleep was further from me than it had been before my ten-and-fifth name day. As it was, staying awake wasn't a challenge at all. The biggest challenge was waiting to make my move until I was fairly certain the others were relaxed enough that I wouldn't draw too much suspicion. Oh, and I'd have to do it before Mad Uncle Ian returned, which could be any time.

Not knowing when my uncle might return, I decided to act sooner than I might have otherwise. The moment I heard all breathing in the room slow, I moved, scrambling over the bed.

"What…"

Connar's voice came out of the darkness as my hands closed on Ian's pack.

"…are…"

I upended the pack, spilling its contents everywhere.

"…you…"

I heard the hollow thunk of my flute hitting the floor.

"…doing?"

Someone dropped from one of the bunks just as I snatched the flute up. Scrambling across the floor, I drew in a deep breath and let loose with a high-pitched note.

The four soldiers cried in pain. The window shattered, blasting outward.

Before the soldiers recovered, I took another breath and started playing a jig. Normally, I'd have just tried putting them to sleep with a lullaby, but that would take far too long, and by "far too long" I mean that it would take more time than it would take for one of them to cross the room and pull the flute away. So…a jig it was. I'd gotten so good with jigs that even before I finished the measures their bodies moved to my music, carrying them out into the hall and away from me. I heard other doors opening in the custom house, followed by cries of surprise and the shuffling and tapping of more feet.

Scrambling out of the window forced me to stop playing for a moment. Footsteps pounded toward me.

When I dropped to the ground outside the window, I started playing again as loud as I could. All the doors in

106

the custom house slammed shut, and the furniture piled in the way of the doors and windows.

Curses from Mad Uncle Ian's soldiers followed me as I ran barefoot into the night. True, I'd left everything but my trousers, shirt, and flute back in that room without ever being able to go back and get them. I left them without a moment of remorse. So long as I had my flute, anything else I might need was replaceable.

I needed to get as far from this town as I could before Uncle Ian found out I was gone. For that I'd need shoes. And maybe a cloak – the night wasn't that warm. Easily done. After that, I had my flute and the road. Aside from that, what else did I really need?

X

Despite all temptations to find an audience to play for, I avoided taverns and inns completely for the next week. I only got close enough to towns to play my flute and have the things I needed dance out across the fields to me. I tried not to enjoy the cries of surprise – sometimes mixed with fear or amusement – as clothes, blankets, boots, and traveling odds and ends flitted away into the fading light of evening.

After that first week, I went into towns large enough that I could move about without creating a stir. I darkened my hair by staining it with a mix of blackberries and river clay, and despite the heat of oncoming summer, I wore several layers of clothes to hide my small stature. It wasn't the best disguise, but it was better than wandering about as myself to set tongues wagging. As much as I felt I should avoid people for at least another week – a month would be better – I needed to put my ear to the stories about me spreading around, stories about Uncle Ian, and about the king's desires for the magical minstrel.

The first town I came to, I discovered what had distracted Uncle Ian and his soldiers enough for me to escape. Parchment posted on signs and doors read, "CALL TO ARMS! For the crime of kidnapping a princess of the realm, Randyl Flynn and his company are now enemies of the realm. Any man who returns Their Majesties' daughter with the head of Randyl Flynn, shall have the princess's hand in marriage as a REWARD."

As I moved about the town, I also heard rumors and tales that both the king and Randyl Flynn were looking for me, or at least, had their men wandering from town to town and village to village looking for me. After hearing these tales for the fourth or fifth time, I left the town. No need to go looking after trouble where no trouble need be looked after...

I wandered, trying to think of what to do, where to go. The king's men looking for me, I could understand. After all the trouble Uncle Ian and his soldiers had gone through to find me and then keep hold of me at the king's command, I didn't think the king would just forget about me. But what interest did I hold for this Randyl Flynn person? Did he want my flute to help protect against the king's knights and soldiers who were certainly looking for him? If I kept playing in inns and taverns, he surely wouldn't forget about me, either. And I'd always be looking over my shoulder, waiting for the moment when Mad Uncle Ian or some agent of Randyl Flynn would appear. I had the suspicion that each would be less cordial with me than the other.

I considered leaving the kingdom altogether, but if what Ian had said about kings was true, then I'd eventually have the same problem once stories about me grew there. As it was, all the kings and queens and lords and ladies in all the neighboring kingdoms in every direction had probably heard of me. So, any solace I found elsewhere would likely be short-lived at best.

Looking back now, I can understand why parents and grandparents do their utmost to keep young men busy. Having nothing to do but wander and think about my situation led to me growing angrier and angrier at the world, Uncle Ian, Randyl Flynn, and even the king. I just wanted to visit a town or village, play my flute and make people happy, maybe make a few coins, and then move on to the next town. Who were they to deny me that? So long as I brought harm to no one, what right had anyone, even a king, to tell me where I might go and how I might ply my trade? By the end of that week, I decided that I refused to allow anyone to tell me how I might or might not make my way in the world.

They would chase me, and eventually find me. But what a merry chase it would be. I was close to being a legend already. Let them come. In doing so, they would make me more than a legend; I would become a myth. The world would remember my name long after I'd gone from it, and I'd make them regret thinking that they could be my masters.

In my youth, I didn't stop to imagine that that might not be a good thing.

XI

A fortnight and a day after I'd escaped Uncle Ian, hair washed and looking like myself once again, I made my way through a good-sized town. I had my hood up so that my hair would not immediately give me away. The town was not so big that it had taverns scattered around. Rather, it was just large enough to have a square – even though circular in construction, people still called it a square, I'd played in one town where it had been a triangle, yet was still referred to as a square – with three taverns and two inns. I'd been playing and making my presence known in this region of the kingdom for five nights. Each night I played, and as I'd traveled, I let people know that I would be at this town on this particular evening, and that it would be a performance unlike any I'd ever played. I'd played here before, and I'd specifically chosen this place for the three taverns and two inns looking at each other around a circular area with a large well in the very center. The street here was cobbled, and the townspeople called it a square.

Normally, two of the taverns and one of the inns had a collection of tables and chairs outside. That night, each establishment had tables filled with people eating and drinking, already enjoying the evening. Many of them looked about, craning their necks and scanning through the crowds milling about, searching for something…or someone. A warm breeze blew through the streets, just enough wind to be pleasant; if you thought about anything else, the wind would vanish from notice. Only a few clouds hung in the sky which was crimson and flames in the west and a deep indigo in the east. Scattered stars winked down. I smiled up at them, as if we held a secret together.

This setting would do; it would do nicely, even better than I'd remembered.

I went to the kitchen door of each place and asked the tavern master or innkeeper for a log from their stores. Every time I asked, each of them, four men and one woman, began to argue. They stopped arguing when I pulled my hood back for just a moment and showed them my flute.

Once I had my five logs, I wove my way through the growing crowd. It seemed that word had spread and that people had come from far and wide to see my grandest performance. When I reached the center of the square, I dropped the five logs to the cobblestones. The clatter caught the attention of those nearby, quieting them. When they looked in my direction to see what the noise was about, I took my cloak off with a sweeping flourish with one hand and held my flute high in the air with the other. The collective gasp that followed my display of showmanship made me smile. I'd been practicing that maneuver.

I stood, unmoving. The people closest to me hushed those further away. Slowly, whispers and shushing noises rippled through the crowd. Soon silence hung in the square. All eyes were fixed upon me. I turned in a wide circle, taking in my audience and searching the edges of the crowd for those I'd meant to draw to me. Here and there I saw people pushing their way toward me through the crowd. I noticed Rolf right away. And I was fairly certain that Connar was coming at me from another angle. I'd have wagered good coin that Uncle Ian had sent Pyrce to come up behind me somewhere. Since I couldn't see Alynn, the newest of them, I expected Uncle Ian had held the young man back just in case something unexpected happened. I wondered if Uncle Ian had bothered to listen to rumors of people looking for me. On that thought, I saw several men moving toward me from the other side of the crowd. They did not look nearly so pleasant as Mad Uncle Ian's men, if that was believable.

Placing the flute to my lips, I began to play.

A quick flurry of high and low notes set the fire aflame, and not just a simple campfire. A pillar of flame rose into the growing night, alerting everyone in the town that I was here and I had started to play.

People cheered.

Both groups of would-be captors began pushing toward me faster. As if that would help them now. I had my flute in my hands and my song floated in the air. No power in creation could stop me.

For a brief moment, I took my flute from my lips, and cried, "Would you dance?"

Another cheer erupted, and I began a jig, light and airy.

The people danced. The entire square broke into joyous chaos.

A few moments later, cries of glee and surprise came from the inns and taverns as firewood danced out through the doors and toward me. I sent these bits of wood rolling, hopping, and skipping across the cobbles, along paths that moved the crowds to thicken around those coming toward me. The jig changed in tempo and melody so that my laughter at their attempts to take me flitted through the air. On some instinctive level, guided by my song, the people danced ever closer to these men, slowing their progress to a near standstill. The logs I guided danced their way to the fire and tossed themselves into the flames. By the end of my jig, I stood next to a roaring bonfire, the flames leaping into the air high above my head.

With this fire dancing and leaping at the command of my flute, I rested a bit easier.

I spun in a circle, looking for my Mad Uncle Ian.

That's when I saw Pyrce nearly through the crowd to my left and when two other men pushed their way into

116

the bare circle of cobblestones around my fire. None of those three men looked remotely pleasant.

I bowed, smiled, and said, "Good evening, gentlemen."

They rushed toward me, drawing weapons. They were fast, I'll give them that. The problem for them was that my music was faster.

My flute came to my lips again. I played a shrill note that dropped low and menacing. A fountain of flame flew from the fire, soared through the air, and surrounded them, trapping all three in a circle of flame.

The crowd cheered again. As I'd hoped, they'd accepted this as a part of my performance.

Looking to the buildings on the edge of the square, I saw Uncle Ian staring at me from a second story window. Even in the last light of day and over this distance, I saw his scowl. Well, maybe I just wanted to see it, but I had no doubt it was there. I grinned in response.

Let Uncle Ian and Randyl Flynn send their men for me. What could they do to me? With my flute and my cunning, I was the master of my fate, and by the end of that night, I would prove it. If not, I would arrange another night, and another — as many as I needed to, on terms set by me — until they left me alone to my music.

And then my masterful scheme unraveled in a way I would never have foreseen in my youth and naiveté.

The two men sent by Randyl Flynn turned toward Pyrce and cut him down. Pyrce tried to fight, but these hard men split apart and came at him from different sides. While their blades were a bit shorter than Pyrce's, they had obviously fought together, and they caught him off-guard by weaving back and forth as they approached. A moment later, Pyrce, smallest of my Uncle's men, lay dead and bleeding on the cobbles, fire reflecting in his glassy eyes.

All movement stopped. The only sound in the whole square was the popping and hissing of the fire.

In truth, I could have stopped it. My music is faster and stronger than any man. Only I'd never considered that something like this might happen. In that moment, I realized all the fear that my Grandmother Elzibeth had lived with since fleeing her village when she had been about my age. Those two men opened me to the evil and cruelty of the world.

"Flute player," someone called from the crowd, breaking the silence. "You will come with us or we will begin killing everyone around us until you do."

Cries of fear sounded throughout the square. People struggled to get away. This led to more fear and cries and shrieks of pain. How dare these men use these people against me? Even as that thought came into my head, I realized I was no better than they. I had placed these people in this danger by thinking that I could use their gathering to my purpose.

I shook my head. I couldn't think. I had only my rage: my rage at them, my rage at myself, my rage at my grandmother Elzibeth for not leaving well enough alone and for carving this flute in the first place, and finally, my rage at the realization that no matter what happened in my life, I would not cast this bloody flute aside. I would play it, I would seek out audiences to play for, and I would use its power. Elzibeth had lasted longer than I, but even she, in the end, had not been able to resist the lure of the flute's power. Knowing I would not cast the flute aside, I might as well use its power to make the world a little safer for those who could not protect themselves from its evils.

I sucked in a deep breath through my nose, and my entire body tensed.

I placed my rage and hatred into my song. Fire leapt from the logs and into the air. I closed my eyes, and as my fingers flew across my flute, the fire spread through the air across the square. The cries and screams of fear lowered to whimpers. Everyone froze in place and cowered beneath the sheet of flames that spread above them. I didn't see so much as felt where the five other men sent by Randyl Flynn slithered through the crowd – that is, five other men besides the two who had killed Pyrce.

The flames engulfed those two first. They screamed as they burned, their flesh popping and hissing even louder than the bonfire had. A moment later, I sent the flames to roast four of the other five of Randyl Flynn's men. That last one, the man who had threatened to cut into the crowd that had wanted nothing more than to be entertained I trapped in a circle of fire. He would not escape. Through the song, I let that man know how much his fellows suffered. And suffer they did. They burned slow, slow and screaming.

One way or another, this night would be a lesson to those who would try to control me, to tame me, a lesson to those who thought they might call me to come heel as they might call a loyal, or in my case a broken, pet. The only way any man might call me to heel was if they found a way to break me. Only, I would not be broken. The elements of the world were mine to command through my song. These men who burned would serve as a warning.

As the men died, I shifted my song from the song of rage to a lullaby, the same lullaby I'd used to escape my home so many months before. How many times would I use this song to protect my freedom?

When everyone in the square was asleep, I stopped playing. My fingers and lips ached. I wobbled on my feet, barely able to keep upright. Only my will and the sight of the man cowering within a scorched circle kept me standing. He was still awake because the fire that roared around him had kept him from hearing my lullaby.

I drew in a ragged breath and started for him.

He looked up at me. His hand went to his sword.

I lifted my flute to my lips and glared at him, daring him, defying him to draw the weapon.

I wonder at the sight I must have made, with the fire roaring behind me, all those people lying in the street, his fellows still smoldering.

"Killian, stop," Uncle Ian said off to my right.

I glanced over to him.

He walked toward me, holding the bone-colored blade out in front of him.

"Stop," I said, without lowering my flute. "Stop… stop…why?"

"Look around," Ian said. "Look at what you've done."

"Me?" I asked. "All I wanted to do was entertain people. Even before you sent me off in search of this thing," I waved the flute at him.

As soon as the flute moved away from my mouth, the other man turned to flee.

"No!" I snapped, bringing the flute back to my mouth in an instant.

I let loose a deep, warbling note. He made it two steps, and then the cobbled street rippled as if it had become water. With a groan, a huge chunk of the street ripped up from the ground and blocked his path.

The man turned to me, his eyes wide, chest heaving, and noticeably, he stretched his arms wide, hands far from his sword. He looked like he didn't plan on running any more. That was good. I was so tired. I just wanted to sleep.

"Killian, please!" Uncle Ian pleaded.

I spun on him. His voice grated on my ears like an out-of-tune instrument. Odd that those two words fueled my fury and burned away my fatigue.

"Please, what?" I demanded. "Now that you've gotten what you wanted from me after sending me to get this thing, you expect me to give it up or become some lapdog to a king, like you?"

"I am no man's lap dog," Ian said.

"You're right," I said. "A lap dog would know the comfort of the king's house. You've been sent to fetch a new toy for the king." My voice grew quiet as I glanced to Randyl Flynn's man. "I will be no one's toy." I fixed my eyes on Ian. "I will not come to heel," I screamed to the sky, "I will not be broken."

"Killian," Ian said. "Let me help you."

"You've done enough," I replied.

Then I played. For the first time since I'd gotten the flute, I played "The Beggar King." As I started the tune that never fails to lift my spirits, Uncle Ian rushed toward me. I played a bit faster, and when he was only a few paces away, I closed my eyes as I completed the chorus.

'I'd rather be a beggar than a king,
And I'll tell you the reason why.
A king can never be free from a beggar,
Nor half as happy as I!"

XII

I finished playing and opened my eyes.

The three-quarter moon shone above. The stars twinkled and winked down at me, sharing our private jest. Moon and stars illuminated the world around me now that true night had fallen. A road wound its way through the hills before me. I squinted, scanning the horizon. I saw no flicker of light anywhere ahead of me save for those in the heavens.

Despite the fatigue that pressed down on me, I smiled. No. Not smiled. I grinned.

"I will not be broken," I cried so loud that broken echoed against the hills around me.

"You play a crafty and dangerous game, little songbird," a voice said above and behind me.

I turned.

The spectral dragon looked down upon me. This time I did not scream. I gave the creature a deep performer's bow.

"And even now, your game continues," the dragon said.

I shrugged. "I don't know any other way to be. I think I did, before you, before the flute. Now, I am just me."

"And who are you?" the dragon cocked its head to the side. "Are you Killian? Are you the magic minstrel? Or, are you someone or something completely different?"

I opened my mouth to reply, but then decided that I didn't have an answer. Who was I? Did I have a choice? And if I did not have a choice, if the flute had changed me, then did it not mean that I was not my own man? Perhaps. Perhaps not. I'd already grown tired of trying to wrap my mind around that particular juxtaposition and the ramifications of what it might mean for me.

"Who can truly tell?" I replied. "Perhaps we are different creatures depending on the moment. Are you a dragon or a specter? Can you be said to be one or the other? Are you the same now as when you died, or even when you were born? We are, all of us, the choices that we make, and some of those choices shape us further down the path of our lives – and I suppose in some cases our deaths. I am who I choose to be."

In speaking those words, I learned something about Grandmother Elzibeth that perhaps no other person realized, except maybe her husband, but I wasn't sure even he knew the depth of her love for him. Elzibeth had loved Frances so completely that she had given up music in her life to be with him. If she'd played at all, on any flute at all, not just the bone-white wonder I'd inherited through strange circumstance, she wouldn't have been able to resist the lure of the flute's power. In that moment, I chose not to give up the music. I loved it too much.

"And what do you choose, little songbird?" the dragon asked.

"I choose to wander," I replied.

After giving the dragon a deep, theatrical bow, I turned and started down the road into the night, the wind and stars my only companions. Tired as I was, I couldn't help but smile. After a short while, I was skipping. My smile grew into a great, wide grin. I pushed the dragon bone flute into my belt and took out the old reed flute I hadn't played since before my ten-and-fifth name day. Holding it and playing it was like a surprise meeting with an old friend in a tavern. My fingers fit to the holes, and I began to play. Only one song seemed appropriate for the moment.

'I'd rather be a beggar than a king,
And I'll tell you the reason why.
A king can never be free from a beggar,
Nor half as happy as I!"

And, in my mind's ear, I heard the girl's voice singing along with my playing. Playing a flute while smirking is not the easiest task in the world, but I managed. After getting halfway through the song, I turned to my left and skipped into the hills. An odd choice, I know, but I felt something waiting for me in that direction.

For now, let me leave you with this picture of me, even if only for a short while. I would let you see me happy, carefree, and with my feet moving me on the path of my choosing. For soon, all too soon, this would change. Oh, would it change. Soon choices made, by myself and others, would lead to a confrontation of arms, and music, and magic.

Yes, see me there in the night, playing joyful and free. Keep that vision in your mind for the dirge is coming, the dragon bone flute's final dirge.

Late in the darkest part of the night, in a town square where dozens upon dozens of people slept a deep, unnatural sleep, where the fires had died to mere ashes, a man, still holding his sword forged of dragon bone, stood looking over the scene he'd had a hand in causing. Did he feel any guilt? Such a thing would be hard to tell by looking at his face, or even by peeking into the man's mind. He was a servant to his Duty, and for men simple things like guilt, pride, compassion, and truth are easily cast aside in the name of Duty.

At last, for the first time since the flute player had vanished right before the man's eyes, the man looked to his fallen comrade. It hadn't been the flute player's hand that had struck the blows to end the lad's life, but the flute player had been the instrument of death. The man with the dragon bone sword would not again underestimate the flute player's power or craftiness.

Behind the man with the dragon bone sword, about thrice as high as that man was tall, a small tear had opened in the air. If the man had not been so distracted and lost in his thoughts, he might have seen the sliver of a reptilian eye looking out through that tear. Had he seen it, he might have understood what it meant, and what danger lurked beyond it. Alas, consumed as he was with his thoughts of the flute player, the man did not see, and so he remained ignorant.

Beyond that small rip in the fabric between the world of men and the world of legends, a deep and ancient laugh rumbled from a deep and ancient throat. Soon, it would be free.

Pleas enjoy this excerpt from
THE LEGEND OF THE DRAGON BONE FLUTE

THE WIDOW

I've been expecting you. Come in. Come in.

I heard down at the well that you're looking for anyone what's had a brush in with the lad with the magic flute. Yes, good master. I've seen him, heard him play, watched with my own eyes the wonders that his playing brings.

The young man came through the village several weeks ago, and as he passed my house, he asked, "Good woman, why do you weep?"

I told him as much as I'll tell you now. My husband joined a militia of men who set about to rescue the princess from the Bandit King, Randyll Flynn. I'm sure you've seen the broadsheets going up in every town, village, and hamlet throughout the kingdom. Save the princess. Become a king. It's like one of those old stories come to life, a grand adventure for them to live out, especially with tales of that lad with the magic flute wandering around reminding them of tales of the fiery-haired lass summoning dragons and cooking knights alive. With their blood spinning about like they were young men, they went off with the plan to rescue the princess. Oh, the ones that were married, such as my husband would be rewarded with some castle or title or something from whichever of the unmarried among them earned the reward of the crown. A few days after the men folk headed out, we find all their heads on sticks just outside of the town. All but one. The eldest of them. Him was tied like a hog and left alive so that he could speak the warning so that no others would seek after such foolishness.

It saddens me to say you can't speak to that man. Even though them bandits left him alive to warn us, they beat him something fierce for his troubles. He didn't last out the week, poor thing.

I told my husband not to go. Begged him. Said we had ourselves a good fine life. Ain't no need for us to seeking to better ourselves when we got so much. When a family has three good fields for growing, a good solid cottage with no leaks in the roof, a sow with a swollen belly, and a cow for milking and her calf for eating or selling, that family has no business looking to reach so high. But some folk, mostly men, the occasional lady, but mostly men can only ever dream of what they have not rather than see the greatness in what they have.

But that wasn't all, next night, we wake up to find our livestock gone or dead. They killed the animals something brutal, with no rhyme nor reason as to which animals they killed, only that they cut them up gruesome and scattered the remains over the whole of the village. I think my sow might have been among them, but can't be sure. The calf definitely was. Found its head on my doorstep. I believe they did lead my cow away, but dead or just gone matters little to me now. The only animals that remained to us were some of the mousers about and the chickens the bandits didn't bother to catch.

So, not only did we grieve for our men, we were force to wonder if we might have enough food to make it through the winter.

And then, though winter is still month upon month away, our troubles continued a few nights later because of our winter snows. You seem like a well-traveled man, with your worn cloak, dusty boots, and that great sword on your back. I'm sure you know of how harsh winters get here in these highlands, not so harsh as those towns up by the Wild Hills up north, but we still see a fair share of snow. More often than not, winter snows cover the windows and doorways. Years and years ago, in the time of I think my grandfather's grandfather, the town determined that they would build chimneys so wide that a man could crawl up trough them, even making a bit of a ladder out of the cobblestones within them. Well, seems them bandits know something of our ways, possibly beaten out of that elder man when they had him prisoner. A few nights later, they got past our barred and locked doors by climbing down the chimneys. Those that were awake, they robbed at knife and sword point, those what slept through the intruder's visit woke to find they no longer had any bit of coin what might have been saved and tucked away. All the money what my husband and I earned and saved by raising swine and cows to sell at market year by year gone. Every penny. Every crown. With it gone, I could not pay the rents when come midsummer.

So that's the story I told the lad as he comes wandering by my cottage two days later. At that point, I found myself wondering when it was they'd come and burn my cottage with me in it.

"Dry your tears good woman," the boy said, as he say down next to me.

He reached into his pockets, and when he brings his hand out again, he shows me a small pile of gleaming silver coins.

"I don't know how much you lost," the young man said as he put them into my hand, "or the price your lord demands for rents, but they are yours."

I tried to decline, thanking him, but he refused to take them back.

"I'll just earn more at the next town I go to."

"I must give you something in exchange," I said to him.

He smiled at me. It's been a long while since a man smiled at me that warmly.

"Three nights," he said. "I'm tired of traveling. You remind me of my mother, though she was a tavern hostess rather than a farmer, but still. Give me a few meals, what ever you can, and a dry place to rest, and we'll call it a bargain true. Otherwise, I'll be on my way without taking the coin back."

So, I agreed. I cooked him meals. He slept on a pallet by the fire. All the while, he remained warm and sweet. Every moment, he remained warm and friendly.

The morning after the first night, I woke to him playing his flute just outside the door. He stood facing the distant mountains, leaning forward a bit, as if trying to send his song specifically in that direction. The song went on and on until I had prepared breakfast. I tell you, sir, his playing helped ease my heart as it ached for my husband, and my stomach as it turned in worry in thinking about the long, hungry winter I had to face alone. In the evening, he played for near on an hour as the sun set. Again, he faced East, leaning toward the mountains.

The second morning was the same. The young man played and played, and just as the breakfast porridge finished boiling, I heard cries of surprise from outside the cottage.

I rushed outside and found a parade of animals coming through the village. In the midst of that odd, mismatched herd, I saw my cow and sow. Yes, I knew what they looked like. I tell you, sir, that a farmer knows the look of their animals, this one especially. So I tell you, truth and honor, that I saw my cow and sow. As we stared and gaped in shock and wonder, each animal went to it's own pen and stood waiting to be fenced in again.

What? No disbelief? No ridicule? No scoffs at the impossibility of it all? Not even a snicker of contradiction. Well then, you certainly are a surprise. Ah, you've seen him before. That would explain your interest. I thought you might be just hunting rumors. You aren't the first.

The first group of bandits came through looking for the large, fair-haired lad what played the flute a few days after our livestock returned. You heard me true. I said, "large, fair-haired lad," and I meant, "large, fair-haired lad." In the time since the lad come and go, I've heard talk of the scrawny lad of flaming hair. I've also heard that it was the read-headed lass come back from across the years. Even heard tell it was Randyll Flynn himself what took up the flute for to try to win the heart of the princess fair.

Plenty of rumors whispering about in people's ears, but the truth I know is the fat lad with hair the color of straw come to this village, play that flute, and our livestock come back to us.

He played one more time, the night after our livestock come home. All through the night he played. I sat with him and listened, for deep down I knew this would be the last I'd hear him, and I so loved his playing. It made me forget all of my woes and sorrows, if only for a short while.

Round about midnight, I see shadows and dark moving between the houses. I nearly jumped up and ran into my house. What else could it be but bandits back for some new malicious mischief? The lad's song stopped me. As his fingers danced on that instrument, I could almost hear the commands coming from it, almost as if the music had become words. "Bother these people no more. They have suffered enough. They have nothing for you. You'll find no profit here. Tell your fellows." For hours and hours, from that darkest hour of the night through the wee hours of the morning and into dawn, the lad played, and those bandits stood transfixed until the sun shone its light over the western horizon, and then they wandered off unto whence ever they come.

The lad stayed long enough for breakfast before leaving. Only liberty he ever took with me was to kiss my cheek just a fore taking his leave. Good lad. Sweet and kind.

Didn't I tell you?

Oh, I suppose I lost myself in the telling of the story.

"Samal," he said when I asked his name, "but my friends call me, Sam."

I'm sure. Not Killian. He never spoke of or mentioned a Killian. I never thought to ask him where he was from or how he came by the flute. I was just so grateful for his music and his favor I only thought to ask him how he came to be so kind.

"I learned my manners from my mother," he said. "She helped keep a tavern, and I saw all manner of men there. I decided I didn't want to be the sort of man my mother would complain about."

I hope whatever is the reason you seek him, should you find him, that you treat him decent. If you mean him ill, I hope you never find him. If you're a man of honor, I hope you protect the lad from the world.

ABOUT THE AUTHOR

M Todd Gallowglas is a master of toast, though he prefers Poptarts (blueberry, unless it's s'mores slathered with Nutella) and plain bagels (he has through astounding levels of self-discipline overcome his pizza bagel issues). Somehow, he gets all the right answers despite asking all the wrong questions, except those answers also don't match the questions he's asking. Every book he writes is an attempt to match the answers to the correct and corresponding questions. His Celtic rock themed Taylor Swift cover band is named Moist Shenanigans, and you can catch them playing in the Korova Milk Bar, Callahan's Place, and McAnally's Pub.

Made in the USA
Columbia, SC
06 September 2021

44972635R00076